TRUTH NOT POETRY

Skye Fargo figured Thomas Bradford was just a crazy poet who did nothing more violent than spout ridiculous rhymes about loving noble savages.

That was before Skye barely dodged Bradford's knife, only to have the writer's nonsense-filled head ram deep into Skye's gut.

Bradford was astride Fargo now, his hands clamped on the Trailsman's neck. The poet's lips drew back, baring his teeth like a ravaging wolf, as he tightened his stranglehold.

"Why, you son of a bitch," Fargo rasped, seeing red as he clenched his fist.

Bradford had switched from words to action and Skye Fargo didn't mind doing the same. He wasn't aiming to wash out the poet's mouth anymore—he was going to clean his clock . . .

THE TRAILSMAN 78

MINNESOTA
MISSIONARY

by
Jon Sharpe

A SIGNET BOOK

NEW AMERICAN LIBRARY

NAL BOOKS ARE AVAILABLE AT QUANTITY DISCOUNTS WHEN USED TO PROMOTE PRODUCTS OR SERVICES. FOR INFORMATION PLEASE WRITE TO PREMIUM MARKETING DIVISION, NEW AMERICAN LIBRARY, 1633 BROADWAY, NEW YORK, NEW YORK 10019.

The first chapter of this book previously appeared in *Devil's Den*, the seventy-seventh volume in this series.

SIGNET, SIGNET CLASSIC, MENTOR, ONYX, PLUME, MERIDIAN AND NAL BOOKS ARE PUBLISHED BY NAL PENGUIN INC., 1633 BROADWAY, NEW YORK, NEW YORK 10019

First printing, June, 1988

1 2 3 4 5 6 7 8 9

PRINTED IN THE UNITED STATES OF AMERICA

The Trailsman

Beginnings . . . they bend the tree and they mark the man. Skye Fargo was born when he was eighteen. Terror was his midwife, vengeance his first cry. Killing spawned Skye Fargo, ruthless, cold-blooded murder. Out of the acrid smoke of gunpowder still hanging in the air, he rose, cried out a promise never forgotten.

The Trailsman they began to call him all across the West: searcher, scout, hunter, the man who could see where others only looked, his skills for hire but not his soul, the man who lived each day to the fullest, yet trailed each tomorrow. Skye Fargo, the Trailsman, the seeker who could take the wildness of a land and the wanting of a woman and make them his own.

Spring, 1862. Fort Laramie, Nebraska Territory.
The Indians remain generally peaceful, but
a general is on the warpath. His daughter
has vanished in distant Minnesota,
among the Santee Sioux. . . .

1

While the gray clouds overhead took their sweet time in deciding whether to provide icy sleet, April blizzards, or maybe even a twister, Skye Fargo hastened toward Fort Laramie. Surrounded by the loneliest stretches of the Nebraska Territory, the fort was the last major military outpost on the Oregon Trail before the staggering Rockies. But Fargo wasn't riding the trail.

For several days he had been traversing the high plains. A beautiful but stark land, it belonged to the sagebrush, the antelope, the jackrabbits, the rattlers, and the wind. Mostly the wind. A tenacious landlord who didn't take kindly to trespassers, the wind beat at Fargo, forcing his head down so he couldn't even enjoy the scenery.

The land roughened as it dipped toward the Platte. Fargo wended his way through forested hills and stark bluffs. The raw, damp wind followed him, crooning a melancholy tune, but it wasn't as strong as it had been.

The fort was an impressive village, bigger than most towns in the West and much better outfitted, with its stores, housing, stables and offices, laundry, blacksmith shop, telegraph office, post office, and hospital. Even so, the famous fort where the Laramie River joined the North Platte had an abandoned feel when Fargo arrived. Nowadays, there were many fewer men at the fort than there once had been, and it was still too early in the season for the freight and emigrant trains leaving St. Joe to have swollen the population. The Trailsman left his big Ovaro stallion with the remount officer and followed a soldier across the deserted parade ground.

The two-story headquarters was downright cold inside, as if the folks at the fort were letting themselves be misled into thinking that the weather was improving by the few tufts of emerald sprouting on the parade grounds. No heat seemed to be radiating from anywhere, and many windows were open. Through the gaping doorway of an empty office, Fargo viewed an open window dubiously.

"General Colson's idea," Fargo's young escort explained. "He says fresh air is conducive to clean, fresh thoughts."

"Probably works," Fargo agreed. "If you want to spend your time thinking about frostbite and exposure."

Oblivious to both the cold and the two men who had just stepped into his office, Major Jacob Whitcombe ran his hand through his hair as he scowled down at a report. The major's coffee cup was empty, his ashtray was full, and the forgotten cigar he held in one hand was just about to burn the tips of his fingers.

"Major Whitcombe, sir?" Fargo's escort interrupted.

Startled, the major glanced up. Fargo couldn't remember having ever seen an army officer who looked so dazed, except maybe once down in New Mexico when the troops were out of water and the Apache were closing in. Whitcombe's blue coat was tossed aside, his shirt sleeves were rolled up, and he definitely needed a shave.

"Damn," Whitcombe muttered as his cigar made its presence known.

"You asked to see Mr. Fargo immediately," the young soldier ventured uncertainly, visibly chagrined at having caught his commanding officer in such a glory of sloth.

But after blowing on his fingers, Whitcombe managed to recover some of an officer's dignity. "Of course," he snapped perfunctorily. "You're dismissed, Private Rand."

Whitcombe was on the short side and husky, but his bulk was trim and muscular. He looked like he'd be damned competent in a fight. Knowing the army, Fargo figured that's why they had the major inside shuffling papers. There were Indians out there, raiding the mail route, running off stock, harassing the stage stations. But the major was up to his neck in paperwork.

Whitcombe had the look of a man who had been awake for several days and expected to go sleepless several more. As he came around the desk, extending his hand, Fargo suppressed a grin. Here was a man who tolerated paperwork about as well as he did.

"Skye Fargo," Major Whitcombe greeted him, smiling as he gave Fargo a quick, firm handshake. "I'm glad you're here." The major glanced back at his desk, laughing apologetically. "In spite of the way things look."

"It seems I arrived at a bad time," Fargo suggested, having no idea why he'd been sent for at all. The army had scouts aplenty, half-breed scouts, Indian scouts, army scouts. None was as famous as the Trailsman, but even Skye Fargo himself would admit that three or four of them together just might do an equal job.

"Oh, no," Whitcombe denied, pulling a chair forward for Fargo. The major plucked a huge stack of papers off the desk, hesitated, looked around, and finally dropped the pile on the floor. Several more followed until at last it was possible for the two men to sit down and see each other over the desktop. "Actually, these are all for you," Whitcombe announced, waving toward the stacks of reports now residing on the floor.

"I hope you don't expect me to read all that," Fargo protested. "I'm not much for reports."

Major Whitcombe laughed. "You don't have to be. The army is very much for reports. And it would seem they produce enough for us all. I certainly don't expect you to read them all—since a few of them should give you the idea." Studying Fargo as he leaned back in his chair, Whitcombe commented, "I've heard a lot about you. Your courage, your honesty, your integrity. I assume I can trust you not to repeat anything I say here?"

"That depends," Fargo answered coolly.

"Oh what?"

"On what you say." Fargo shrugged. "If the army's doing something I think folks should know about, I don't feel I've got any obligation to keep it quiet."

The major sighed and nodded, then stared at Fargo for several moments before he spoke. "Well, I suppose I'll just have to trust you anyway," he admitted. Still eyeing Fargo speculatively, Whitcombe leaned over and grabbed a handful of papers. "Here, you look at these," he ordered.

Fargo perused the papers, but he couldn't make head or tail of them. "What is this stuff?" he exclaimed incredulously.

"Bullshit," the major answered readily. "Would you like some coffee?"

Fargo nodded abstractedly as he leafed through the reports. "Poetry?" he muttered.

"The collected writings of one Thomas Bradford," Whitcombe announced as he stepped out of the office.

"What are these dates and names for?" Fargo questioned several minutes later when Whitcombe returned with two cups of coffee.

"The places and times Bradford has lectured. Or in some cases the dates and names of literary publications his works have appeared in."

"All of that can't be Bradford's work," Fargo objected, gesturing toward the stacks of paper.

"You're absolutely right," Whitcombe agreed, handing Fargo another fistful of papers.

There were maps. There were train and stage schedules. There were letters, letters signed by different people but fastidiously copied in the same hand.

"I don't understand," Fargo admitted.

"That's because nobody can," Whitcombe pronounced seriously as he settled back into his chair and lit another cigar. "It seems this Thomas Bradford has become a hobby for a man who's visiting us now, Major General Isaiah Colson. Apparently the general saw Bradford lecture five or six years ago in St. Louis, and he hated him."

"That's a bit foolish, isn't it? Collecting all this stuff if he can't stand the writer. At least I assume this is General Colson's stuff?"

"You're right. They're General Colson's reports. Although they were gathered at government expense, of course."

"Why?"

"Because General Colson wants to see Bradford hanged," Whitcombe answered solemnly, and in such a

12

way that it left no doubt that he meant the statement literally.

"What's this Bradford done?" Fargo blurted, glancing back down at the reports on his lap. Fargo figured this Bradford was a pretty bad poet, but that didn't seem to be a good enough reason to hang him.

"If you read those papers closely you'll see that Bradford can be a bit incendiary, preaching that the Indian is Rousseau's natural man and thus distorted by the white man's encroachment. And being a follower of Emerson, Bradford believes the Indians are too akin to nature to be anything but higher mortals. And apparently Bradford also read Thoreau's eulogy of John Brown's revolt at Harper's Ferry and thus found his mission in life."

"I had enough trouble understanding Bradford's poetry," Fargo accused sourly. "Now I don't understand you."

Whitcombe laughed heartily. "In short, Bradford goes around lecturing that the Indians should be free, and whether it takes letters to Congress or outright war we should all be on the Indians' side."

"So that's what he was trying to get at," Fargo muttered. "Seems there should have been a simpler way to put it."

Skye Fargo frowned back down at the reports, stopping to read one of Bradford's poems more carefully.

> Natural poet, cling to your tepee walls
> The transcendent eye will guide you
> Until the white man falls
> Barbarian Eve, arm yourself to win
> You are one with nature's Unity
> Ideal Knowledge precludes sin

Fargo started reading it, but the poem went on and on, five pages worth, all about sun-kissed braves and maids taking up the lance, the bow and the war club, while somehow still basking in the idyllic pastimes of earthbound but sky-seeking children.

It was so preposterous that Fargo was sure someday they'd be making schoolchildren read it. He had a theory that they always fed you the worst rubbish in school so that the teachers would look smarter. Although school-teachers could be pretty idiotic, Fargo had never met one as bad as this Bradford fellow.

"Well, what difference does it make?" Fargo shrugged. "There's lots of crazy people saying and writing lots of crazy things."

"My point exactly," Whitcombe enthused, jumping out of his chair. "But we have orders to arrest Bradford."

"For talking or for writing?" Fargo asked sarcastically.

"For gunrunning, selling whiskey to the Indians, and encouraging revolt. And for treason," Whitcombe added, almost as an afterthought. The major swooped down and came up with several more papers. Perching on the edge of his desk, he waited tensely while Fargo read them. "Well, what do you think?" Whitcombe asked cautiously when Fargo looked up.

"This stuff looks pretty flimsy," Fargo mused. "Being in St. Louis at the same time as a man later arrested for gunrunning? Then this thing about Indians getting drunk after attending his lecture outside Fort Kearney. And what about this charge of touring the Pawnee Reservation four months before two Indians were arrested for having a private arsenal of government-issued revolvers? Maybe I remember it wrong, but wasn't it two half-breed Cheyenne who were found with those guns?"

"Yes."

"Major Whitcombe, are you implying that Bradford is being framed?"

"No." Whitcombe took a puff off his cigar before he went back to sit down, not seeming to know quite how to proceed.

"You're not going to ask me to go after Bradford, are you?" Fargo demanded as the alarm crept over him. He didn't care if the idiot was throttled. But hanged?

"No. Hell, no," Whitcombe objected. Hesitating, he eyed Fargo uncertainly. "Well, the truth is, we've got a problem here," he admitted. "And unfortunately the problem outranks me. General Colson came out on an

14

inspection tour of the Western forts, and suddenly he up and ordered us to arrest this Bradford for treason.''

Major Whitcombe stood up and took to pacing with his broad shoulders hunched and his solid muscles tensed. Fargo knew Ft. Laramie was running on half staff due to the war back East. There weren't enough men to do much more than chase off marauding Indians. There certainly weren't enough men to post them at the beleaguered stage stations. And this man, who Fargo judged would be both cool and effective in action, was being tortured by bureaucracy.

Having just returned from New Mexico, where an Apache named Cochise, along with his father-in-law, Mangus Colorado, were definitely stirring things up, Fargo reckoned that these Plains tribes were merely being fractious in comparison. But Fargo sure couldn't figure out why an officer at Laramie was wasting his time reading poetry, and he only needed to look at Whitcombe to see the major agreed. The Apache had a habit of hanging a man upside-down over a fire and slowly roasting his brains out. From the look of Major Whitcombe, he could have taken that kind of torture easier.

The major halted his pacing and glared at Fargo. ''God damn it, Fargo, do you know what it's like having an Inspecting General permanently on your ass? The man's got everyone around here spitting and polishing, polishing and spitting, walking on eggshells, saluting shadows.''

Fargo tried to summon up sympathy, but there was a reason he wasn't a military man and never would be. Skye Fargo stretched out his long, buckskin-clad legs and eyed the major. The army meant taking orders and accepting other men's discipline. It always had, it always would, and Whitcombe had known that before he'd ever gotten into it. Like most military men, Fargo thought wryly, the major was better at giving shit than taking it.

''General Colson was supposed to stop here for a weekend and then move on,'' Whitcombe complained, as he began pacing once again. ''But it seems he has a daughter, a preacher's widow, a sort of unofficial missionary to the Santee Sioux in Minnesota. On his way

15

out here Colson stopped at Fort Ridgely, hoping to see her. But the woman is missing. No one's seen her. Well, Colson kept on with his tour, waiting for word. But none came. Apparently, nobody's heard from her. And Colson is stalled right here, refusing to go another mile, claiming that it's military incompetence that made it possible for his daughter to just up and disappear.''

Whitcombe came back and sat down in his chair. ''Colson insists the Sioux took his daughter,'' he continued. ''Fort Ridgely officials say that's nonsense. Their Sioux have been peaceful. One of the officers there, a Captain Bannister, wrote that he knew Mrs. Frasier, that's her name, and he suspects she went back East. Apparently, she had been talking about it. But her father says she's dead.'' The major paused and shook his head, appearing lost in concentration.

''And what do you think?'' Fargo urged.

''I don't know. I think the general might be right. She could have been taken by the Sioux. The funny thing is, nobody wants to look for the woman. I was hoping that if we found her, the general might mellow a bit. But I have this terrible feeling that if she's with the Sioux, he doesn't want her back.''

''Some people feel that way,'' Fargo murmured. His eyes met Whitcombe's, and he knew they were both thinking the same thing. Female captives were usually treated barbarously—raped, beaten, shared, tortured and often purposefully scarred. Even if a woman became the property of one man, she would have no family, no position, and almost certainly no acceptance. And yet sometimes captives survived for years. The general certainly knew that. For him to not even want to look for his daughter seemed exceptionally cruel.

''So, what do you want me to do?'' Fargo asked.

''First, I want you to meet Colson.''

''What for?''

''Well, frankly, I think the general's got a few screws loose. Look, Fargo, General Colson plans on having us arrest Bradford here. After a lecture Bradford has scheduled in Denver in the fall, he's arranged to come to Fort Laramie. Fortunately, right now Bradford is rumored to be taking time off right here in Nebraska someplace to commune with nature or some such thing. What I want you to do is find Bradford and warn him not to show up.''

"That doesn't sound too hard," Fargo commented.

"You do realize that what I'm asking you to do isn't exactly legal? And it definitely isn't according to regulations.''

"Yep," Fargo agreed, and his lake-blue eyes gleamed with amusement. "But then I figured before I ever got here that what you wanted me to do might not be real proper. Otherwise, you would have gotten a regular army scout.''

"You do understand that it's me asking you? Not the U.S. Army. Not the post commander. Me, Jacob Whitcombe. There are others who know about it, but if it's found out, I'll take sole responsibility. To be honest with you, you might be questioned. Hopefully you wouldn't be implicated. But we are talking treason, which is punishable by death.''

"Sounds all right," Fargo assented.

"Good. I'd like you to find the daughter too if you can. But that's not all.''

Fargo smiled knowingly. "I didn't figure it was. You're a mite cautious.''

"Of course I am. General Colson is talking about treason. I have a lot of trouble seeing how Colson came up with that charge, but he says Bradford is trying to help the Indians reclaim two U.S. states, Kansas and Minnesota. Plus he claims Bradford's jeopardizing the functioning and peace of several U.S. territories. And on top of that he claims all of it is for Bradford's own personal gain—which somehow includes establishing a naturalist, transcendental utopia where men can be taught a perfectionist means of existence by the native inhabitants. I suppose Bradford has said all that, but it's just plain drivel.''

Drivel maybe, but Fargo couldn't help laughing when he considered a new tribe of delicate New England palefaces riding off in war paint to count coup on their neighbors.

"Do you know what it will mean if Bradford is arrested?" Whitcombe protested, scowling at Fargo's show of humor.

"I can figure it out," Fargo told him, but Major Whitcombe stormed on without even noticing Fargo's acquiescence.

"Bradford's an easterner," Whitcombe raged. "He's *met* Thoreau and Emerson. He's moderately well-known. Can you imagine the publicity? Not that I really believe that Bradford would get hanged. Although stranger things have happened, it would take a court-martial and I can't see Colson's evidence standing up to that. But the precedent? What kind of precedent would we be setting?"

Whitcombe didn't wait for Fargo to answer; he surged on, "Next thing you know, we'd be arresting Thoreau—which might make more sense anyway, since more people have read his work. Maybe if Thoreau wanted to ride with the Indians he'd actually have some influence," Whitcombe scoffed bitterly.

"And you saw those hoked-up charges," Whitcombe bristled. "Everyone and their horse is going to think it's a crime to attend lectures or church services with Indians. Or to speak to Indians. Or to be seen in the same city with Indians. Indian relations are bad enough right now."

"You can stop trying to convince me and tell me what you want," Fargo objected, his lake-blue eyes sparkling with mirth. "I'd already thought of all that, anyway."

"But it gets worse," Whitcombe insisted.

And Fargo couldn't help but think that once Whitcombe lost his reticence about talking, he was harder to shush than a braying jackass.

"Colson wasn't content to compile charges against Bradford; now he's compiling a report on the Sioux, and on Fort Ridgely and Fort Kearney and Fort Laramie and Fort Randall and Fort Abercrombie. Whether it was really done by angry husbands, jayhawkers, or desperadoes, Colson is crediting the Sioux with all the unsolved murders and mayhem from Minnesota to Kansas and from Iowa to the Rockies. And he's accusing the forts of gross neglect of duty and recklessly endangering the lives of citizens.''

Whitcombe paused to catch his breath. Practicing a little control, he still barely managed to keep his heartfelt sigh from sounding like a stifled roar. ''I think Colson's crazy,'' Whitcombe said a bit more calmly. ''In the end, I'm sure everyone will think he's crazy. But only after innumerable inquiries, court-martials, investigating commissions and full-length reports—which just might take years. But that's the way the army works.''

''Or doesn't work,'' Fargo added, smiling. And he kept smiling, hoping to dispel the bleak expression on Whitcombe's face. The major wasn't only harried, he'd been hounded right into a corner. Whether he was loving it or finding fault with it, Major Whitcombe was obviously an army man from beginning to end, and it was clear he feared the end was near.

''Fargo, I'd like you to meet the general and see what you think,'' Whitcombe murmured, before he smiled in embarrassment, showing that he knew full well how carried away he was getting. ''General Colson's been more than a little difficult to have around looking over everyone's shoulder, and I think maybe we're all acting a trifle crazy here. I'd value your opinion.''

''All right,'' Fargo acknowledged. ''So, you want me to meet the general. Then you want me to wander around Nebraska until I find a poet—so I can tell him to stay lost. And afterward I'm supposed to arrange a little side trip to Minnesota to look for a woman who is either anywhere in Minnesota or Dakota, or anyplace back East. I hope you pay well, Major.''

Major Whitcombe leaned down and took a money bag out of his bottom desk drawer. It looked heavy enough to make Fargo sit up and take notice. ''I thought you'd prefer silver,'' the major told him.

Sure as hell, he'd prefer silver, Fargo thought as he opened the bag and eyed the contents. What with Yankee greenbacks and Confederate money and with every little bank in Nebraska, Kansas, and Minnesota putting out its own scrip, there were more kinds of money going around these days than a man could count. And there was surely so much of the stuff that it wasn't worth anything.

"We'll match it, when your job is completed," Whitcombe assured Fargo.

"You've got yourself a deal," Fargo announced. He didn't stop to count it, but there had to be five hundred silver dollars. He smiled broadly. "What's a little charge of treason compared to this? Men have sold their souls for less."

Whitcombe paled. "I'm sure it won't go that far," he protested. "Treason is a hanging offense."

"Actually, Major Whitcombe, I was under the impression that the army used a firing squad," Fargo told him calmly. "But then again, maybe they give you a choice."

2

Fargo liked the land east of Fort Laramie. It was good riding country, wide open, rolling and smelling earthy with spring. But half the towns on the map didn't exist. There was little wonder as to the cause for all the fictional settlements. Prairie land was going for $1.25 an acre, while a good town lot brought $125.

Only a year or so earlier, the Nebraska Territory had been the largest piece of property in the West. But last year the powers in Washington had given part of it to the new Colorado Territory and cut off the whole top for the new Dakota Territory. It was the same land, but it felt different. All that cutting and reorganizing gave Fargo a feeling that the whole damned West was being eyeballed by greedy easterners.

These days, the Plains were full of promoters, hucksters, wildcat bankers, road ranchers, and anxious folks eager to claim their inexpensive piece of the prairies. There was something wearying about coming back to a familiar place and finding it changed, even if it wasn't anywhere close to being the civilized place that the promoters advertised. But that was the way the West was— always changing.

Once the Plains had been packed with frolicking antelope, migrating buffalo, and great herds of elk. There weren't nearly as many buffalo now, and the Indians were a lot less friendly. Tiny patches of newly planted corn and a few dozen overpromoted but underdeveloped towns, plus a lot of little sod houses and ugly frame shacks, hardly made an impression on the Great Plains, yet. But only eight years earlier, when all of this had still been Indian territory, those things hadn't been there at all.

Thomas Bradford's piece of the prairies sat about three miles away from a fledging town. Pretty fancy as such places went, it boasted a real log cabin in a land where wood was rare. Glancing behind him as he waited on the Ovaro, Fargo could see across at least two miles of open grassland. It grew hardier and thicker than it did farther west, but there wasn't a tree in sight.

As Fargo rode up on the Ovaro, a man stepped onto the porch. Looking more like a sapling than a mighty oak, Bradford was tall and gaunt. Lean-faced, he resembled President Lincoln, except Bradford hadn't reached thirty yet and appeared even younger. A few character lines would have sat well on him.

Fargo swung down from the pinto, strode to the porch, and got right to the point. "Mr. Bradford, I came to inform you that you're wanted for treason."

"Excuse me, sir?"

"I've come from Fort Laramie to tell you that you're wanted for treason," Fargo repeated nonchalantly. "But I'm not here to arrest you."

Taller than Fargo by an inch or so, but at least fifty pounds lighter, Bradford was as skinny as a telegraph pole. He swayed slightly and his long, thin fingers reached out to grasp the door frame. After a minute of gawking speechlessly at Fargo, he nodded vaguely and went back into his cabin. Since the door was still open, Fargo followed him inside.

"Treason?" Bradford whispered. "Are you entirely certain, Mr. . . . ah?"

"Fargo. Skye Fargo. You are Thomas Bradford? The poet who's been trying to incite the Indians?"

"Why, yes, I am," Bradford admitted. Looking stunned, he sank onto a chair at the kitchen table.

The kitchen was neat and tidy, in spite of the books and papers littering the table. The sink boasted a hand pump, and all of the dishes and pots and pans in the house were washed, dried, and stacked in an open cupboard next to the woodstove. For a two-room cabin, the

22

kitchen was fairly roomy, and it boasted an enviable amount of wooden counterspace.

A red-flowered curtain hung at the back of the kitchen, presumably closing off the bedroom, and a matching curtain covered a real glass window, which was positioned just right so a man could look through it as he dined. Outside darkness was just beginning to descend on prairie grasses that were just starting to green with spring.

Looking around, Fargo decided he wouldn't mind having a little retreat just like this one. It was cozy and comfortable, and he was tired after a week of riding around Nebraska making inquiries. On the other hand, considering half the towns he'd ridden off to find hadn't existed, he felt pretty good about finding Bradford so soon.

"There any coffee in that pot?" Fargo asked, gesturing toward the fancy four-lid woodstove, where the fire was dampered down just enough to take the chill out of a cool evening.

"What? Oh, yes." Although he was still a little pale, Bradford seemed to be coming around. "There's coffee."

Fargo sauntered over and poured himself a cup. When he turned back, Bradford was staring up at him with an odd, dazed smile playing on his lips. Bradford didn't look so bad when he smiled. The lean, smooth-shaven cheeks looked almost boyish, and the dark brown, long-lashed eyes radiated the same kind of sad but eager look a puppy might bestow.

"You all right?" Fargo muttered, turning back again to pour Bradford a cup of coffee.

"I never felt anyone took me seriously," Bradford answered.

"Well, I wouldn't get too excited about it," Fargo cautioned, seeing the man was doing just that. Bradford's bony fingers trembled as they encircled his coffee cup. "I came to warn you, not arrest you," Fargo said. "If you lie low for a while, and don't go to Fort Laramie in the fall, you should be just fine."

"I can't do that," Bradford protested.

"Why not?" Fargo demanded, although he already

23

knew by the dopey smile spreading across Bradford's face that the man was warming to the idea of being wanted for treason. Apparently it made Bradford feel important.

"I have a mission, Mr. Fargo. Perhaps you are unfamiliar with my work, but . . ."

"I've read some of it," Fargo interrupted.

"Really?" Bradford positively beamed. "Then you must understand how this can be an opportunity to spread my word. I have several articles scheduled to appear in eastern journals. Surely they'll be of much more interest after I'm arrested."

"And you'll be in prison," Fargo reminded him.

"You've heard of Mr. Thoreau? He too went to prison—to protest taxes destined to support the Mexican War. His decision to be imprisoned rather than intimidated highlighted his cause. There are many who respect his action."

"I'm sure there are. But treason carries the death penalty," Fargo offered placidly.

Bradford blanched. "You're quite certain?" he murmured.

"Yep."

"Well—" Bradford faltered. After several moments he mustered his courage. "It's what I have to do. You can take me in now, sir. I'm ready."

"I'm not taking you in," Fargo objected.

"Perhaps that's for the best," Bradford assented. "You implied they would arrest me if I went to Fort Laramie. I'm supposed to speak there in the fall. That will give me time to prepare several articles. And if their publication coincides with my arrest, my message should attain a generous audience. Yes," he murmured. "Yes, it should work out quite well."

Fargo frowned. This was supposed to have been an easy job. All he had to do was ride out, find Bradford, and tell him that if he showed up at Fort Laramie he'd get hanged or shot or drawn and quartered or something equally unpleasant. If the man wasn't a complete idiot he'd stay hidden for a while. Unfortunately, Bradford was a complete idiot.

"You're crazy," Fargo chafed. "I read that stuff of

24

yours. You want a lot of poets and writers and ladies to come out and live like Indians. But Indians know how to live hard. Indians thrust skewers under their ribs. They take long evil-looking shafts of bone tied to rawhide and dangle on them till their muscles rip apart—just so they can show they're men. Their women slash themselves with knives when they mourn. Indians bathe in icy steams, run naked in blizzards, and eat raw liver. They have lice, for God's sake.''

"You think I'm naive, don't you, Mr. Fargo? I'm aware that the Indians indulge in ceremonies celebrating self-inflicted pain. I also know they partake in ritualistic warfare. They scalp and torture and murder. But is that as destructive as the war the white man currently inflicts on his children?'' Bradford stared up at Fargo, his dark eyes intent. "You say the white man can't live as Indians. But they'll just have to learn,'' Bradford pronounced angrily. "It is the salvation of man. His only salvation. To learn to live with nature and through nature,'' he finished flatly.

Fargo knew better than to argue with him. Men like Bradford could always spout enough to drown your point. He'd brought along some of Bradford's work, and he'd spent days on the trail perusing it, since it paid to know the man you were tracking. But it was a good thing that Whitcombe was paying well, because Bradford's poetry was laborious fare. Some of it was kind of pretty, but all of it was crazy.

"Look, I think it's nice you see something to admire in Indians,'' Fargo hazarded. "They're as much a part of this place as grizzly bears and wolves, and they can be as frightening and as beautiful. But even if I agreed that their way was better, simpler, and more natural, I couldn't live that way. Yet you think a bunch of poets can come out and live that way. That's not an idea worth dying for, Bradford.''

"But it can work,'' Bradford objected. "If I convert enough people to my cause, it has to work. The so-called civilized man seeks enlightenment through knowledge. But he only increases his knowledge of greed and weapons and warfare. Enlightenment must come through nature.'' Bradford was off now, his voice deep, resonant, and trembling with conviction.

Perching a hip against the counter, Fargo folded one arm across his chest and raised the coffee cup to his lips, contemplating the situation as he surreptitiously stretched muscles chastened by six days of riding. It was now clear that he was going to have to come back in the fall and forcibly prevent Bradford from going to Ft. Laramie.

But maybe after the poet had gushed out his sentiments, it would help to scare him with tales of prison and death. Fargo wanted to be sure that Bradford would not go wandering off to Fort Laramie while the Trailsman was in Minnesota searching for General Colson's daughter.

When the curtain behind Bradford was pushed aside, the poet was just building to a crescendo, and it was impressive, like listening to a good church choir—even if you weren't a churchgoing man. But the woman coming into the kitchen was even more impressive, and almost naked.

Fargo raised an eyebrow. The woman was twisted around, fooling with the clasps on the back of the lacy black nothing she was wearing, so he couldn't see her face. But he could see almost all of the rest of her.

''Tommy, could you help me with this?'' she asked.

Forgetting his cause entirely, Thomas Bradford was out of his chair and blocking Fargo's view just as the woman raised her head. ''Annabelle, we have company,'' Bradford chided.

Watching as Bradford attempted to push the woman back into the bedroom, Fargo found himself grinning at Bradford's discomfiture. Until now he had thought Bradford's only passion was his cause.

''I'm sorry, Tommy,'' she apologized. ''I thought you was just practicing your speech-giving.'' The woman's head bobbed out from behind Bradford. ''Skye?'' she squealed. ''Skye Fargo? Is that really you?''

Fargo barely managed to set aside his coffee cup before the woman bounded out from behind Bradford and tumbled into his arms. ''Belle?'' he mumbled, looking down into her shining blue eyes.

26

Belle's cheeks were flushed and her wheat-colored hair was wild. As she shook her head and laughed, the long mass fluffed around her face, billowed across her arms, and latched onto Fargo's shirt buttons. Belle was a tiny little thing with wide, innocent-looking eyes, and she was pretty, real pretty.

But it was the breasts pressed against Fargo's midriff that made Belle damned near famous. Even men who claimed to be connoisseurs of slender legs and shapely rumps couldn't bypass a chance to ogle Belle's bosom. As memorable and impressive as Scott's Bluff and almost as monumental, Belle's bosom was talked about throughout the West, and it had definitely earned her the name Belle DeVista.

"How did you find me?" Belle demanded.

"I didn't," Fargo admitted. "I came here to see Bradford."

"Really? Then I'll bet you're surprised," she exclaimed, her eyes sparkling.

Fargo was so surprised he didn't even glance down at the magnificent cleavage exposed by Belle's black lace corset. And he barely noticed that his hands were resting on her bare shoulders. "I thought you were in Colorado," Fargo said. "That's what Lil told me."

Some of the sparkle faded from Belle's eyes. "I was with Jim DeLacey. You remember Jim, don't you? Jim was having real poor luck in California, but he won a claim in Buckskin Joe. Poor Jim. He lost it again afore we even got there."

"Goddamn it, Belle. I warned you about DeLacey."

"Aw, Skye. Jim ain't so bad. He just ain't much of a card player. And I done fine. Business is real good in them boomtowns."

"What happened to DeLacey?" Fargo asked. The last time he had seen Belle she had been madly in love with Jim DeLacey, although she had still been working—since DeLacey never could hold on to a hard-earned dollar.

"You won't believe it, but Jim's doing fine. Got hisself a mercantile."

"With your money, I'll bet," Fargo railed. Scowling

down at Belle, Fargo gave her time to deny the accusation, but she didn't. "Where's your share, Belle?"

"Jim met hisself a nice little girl," Belle explained defensively. "Just sixteen and real respectable. They got hitched, and he can't afford to pay me back just yet. Besides, you know I don't care about such things." Belle attempted to smile through the tears in her bright blue eyes. Fargo bristled.

"Goddamn it, Belle. You let everybody take advantage of you. When are you going to learn to take care of yourself?"

"Skye, don't do this in front of Tommy," she pleaded.

With effort Fargo bit back his stinging retort. As always, he was glad to see Belle, but he wanted to throttle her, too. He had known her a long time, and her story was familiar to him.

The oldest of ten children born to a Missouri farm family, when she was twelve, Belle had been hired out to relieve her family's overcrowded conditions. Predictably enough, bachelors had been willing to pay her father considerably more for her skills than the average housewife had been. And her father had been too greedy to object.

Not that Belle ever complained, but over years of knowing her, Fargo had gotten a pretty good picture of what those old farmers had been like. Besides, Belle had run off to the city. And that wasn't like her. A lot of girls were real happy whoring. It offered money, freedom, excitement, a constant supply of admirers, and a lot of physical gratifications. But Belle didn't care about those things.

She yearned for something more. And she hankered after every man with a hard-luck story. Belle liked her men best if they needed her sympathy, her love, and her money. Fargo wondered why he'd been so surprised to find her here. If he had thought about it at all, he would have figured on it. Bradford's syrupy poetry alone would enchant her. And his being a scrawny, sad-eyed, rather unlikely sort of Romeo would only heighten his attraction in Belle's eyes.

"Come on, Skye," Belle cajoled. "I'm doing fine. Tommy's teaching me to read. And I made them curtains,'' she added enthusiastically. "And I even planted a garden.''

Belle smiled and her jaw quivered. That was a trait of hers, the way her chin wavered when she smiled, probably because she was always smiling to hide some personal heartache. Wrapping one of her straying curls around his hand, Fargo stroked her cheek with his fingers. Why did she have to be here?

She acted so excited about this place, but he had seen her decked out in satin with ostrich plumes spraying from her hat and rubies glittering around her throat. A few years back, one of Belle's beaus had put her on the stage. Although her singing and dancing hadn't been exceptional, every time she had taken a breath, the miners had buried the stage with coins. But after a few months Belle's beau had taken off with all those coins and Belle had gone back to Miss Lil's.

When she was working, Belle was the strongest attraction Miss Lil could lay claim to, but even Lil got put out with Belle. Lil's was a fancy house with gilded mirrors, velvet curtains, brass spittoons, the whole works. But Belle had never so much as owned a simple gold necklace for more than a month.

Men weren't Belle's only problem. She lent her things to the girls on the line, gave her gold to the fire department, and even wired money to strangers she'd read about in the newspapers. Looking down at the hesitant smile playing across Belle's lips, Fargo wanted to rage at her. But he wasn't any better than any of the other men Belle knew. Whenever their paths crossed, Fargo was nagging her. With his angry outbursts alone, he'd probably brought more tears to her wide blue eyes than anyone else. Belle just made it too damned easy to take advantage of her.

"You're looking good," Fargo admitted. "You've got a lot of color in your cheeks.''

"Is this a private party, or am I invited to join?'' Bradford broke in sarcastically.

Fargo looked up to find Bradford glaring at them. "I'm sorry, Bradford. It's just that it's been awhile since I've seen Belle.''

"Oh, a reunion. Perhaps I had better leave before the two of you are more intimately reunited."

Glancing back down, Fargo realized he was holding a nearly naked woman in his arms, a woman whose breasts swelled lavishly out of the top of her corset. He started to laugh at his oversight until he glanced up again and saw the stricken look on Bradford's face. Bradford's jaw was clenched and his color had dwindled to the point where it had the same kind of chalky, glaucous hue as an alkali flat. He was the closest thing to a man turned green by jealousy that Fargo had ever seen.

"Bradford," Fargo protested. "We're just old friends."

"Really, Mr. Fargo? Well, I suppose old friends need a chance to be alone together. To relive old times, so to speak. The two of you can shut the door behind you when you leave."

Belle whirled, yanking her hair loose from Fargo's buttons. "Please, Tommy," she cried. "It ain't like that." Instinctively Belle folded her arms across her chest, seeming to remember her state of undress for the first time. "Skye and I ain't like that."

But Thomas Bradford glowered rigidly, his face set in an uncompromising scowl.

"Oh, Tommy, I'm sorry," Belle whimpered. "I just didn't think. And Skye? Skye didn't mean nothing." Belle glanced back at Fargo, the tears flowing down her cheeks. "Even when I worked at Miss Lil's, Skye liked Sally better."

That wasn't strictly true. Nobody liked Sally better, but Skye Fargo didn't like paying for sex, and there was no guilt in not paying Sally. Sally took what she could get from a man. If he wasn't offering coin, she took it out in labor.

Fargo studied Belle, knowing Bradford was never going to believe their embrace was innocent. It wasn't entirely innocent. Fargo had been in Belle's bed often enough and he appreciated the territory, the contours, and the scenery as much as any other man.

"I think I'd best be going," Fargo muttered, walking to the door. Pausing, he looked back at the still furious poet. The tall, lanky man towered over Belle. ''Bradford, it might be better if you don't forget you've got a lot more important things to think about and discuss than me. What about those articles you were going to work on? You might never get another chance after this fall.''

3

Resting his elbows on the bar, Skye Fargo glared down into his fifth glass of whiskey and told himself that whatever happened to Belle DeVista was none of his business. If she'd gotten into hot water it was her own fault. Straightening, he picked up the whiskey glass and tossed the contents down his throat.

"Another," he called.

There was a lithograph taped to the mirror behind the bar, a pretty, placid scene of a city built on the bluffs of a river, with a steamboat chugging past. Fargo thought maybe it was an early-day version of St. Louis, but even so it didn't look big enough. Looked a bit like Red Wing, Minnesota. Or maybe Alma, Wisconsin. It seemed about that size. But it had been awhile since Fargo had taken a steamboat. "Where's that?" he asked as the bartender served him.

"Melville Springs," the bartender replied.

"Melville Springs?" Fargo snapped in disbelief. "Nebraska?"

"Yep." The bartender grinned.

"I was just there," Fargo bristled. "Hell, there's nothing there but two shacks leaning out over a creek I could step across."

"It's what the Julius Merstein Development Company calls an artistic rendering," the bartender laughed. "Real artistic, I'd say, but not much in the way of a rendering. They send 'em back East to folks fool enough to invest in town lots, site unseen."

Grimacing, Fargo looked away from the fanciful picture of Melville Springs, and his gaze landed on one of the ubiquitous recruiting posters that decorated saloons everywhere these days. Maybe it was just Belle and Bradford, plus Major Whitcombe and General Colson, not to mention the whole gloomy nature of the folks at Fort Laramie, but the times were getting to him.

The Trailsman had always been a bit of a celebrity at Fort Laramie, but during his last stay everybody had kept treating him like visiting royalty. Whitcombe might have claimed he was solely responsible for Fargo's employment, but everyone at the fort had known why Fargo was there. And they had all been eager to offer their help, maps of Nebraska Territory, maps of Dakota Territory, maps of Minnesota, names of Indians, names of Indian agents. Even if some of them felt Fargo's mission was a long shot, they were all eager to end Colson's reign of terror.

For the life of him, Fargo couldn't figure out how a man who wasn't pointing a gun could make so many people so nervous. But General Colson had everybody at the fort shivering, shaking, and jumping at shadows. Fargo had met the general over dinner. It hadn't been his favorite kind of shindig, with the men in dress uniform and the ladies in their best. Plus there was so much silver that a man didn't dare rest his elbows for fear of spearing himself.

Major Whitcombe's wife, Lieutenant Sanderson's wife, and Captain Smithson's wife had all tried to keep the general talking. Hemming and hawing and beating around the bush, they had asked at least a hundred questions of the poor man, all in the guise of proper small talk. They had interrogated the general about everything from new styles to last year's battles. And probably all of their babbling was only meant to prove to Fargo that the man was crazy.

There was little cause to wonder why the general had grown so grouchy. Those women would have driven anyone to distraction.

And the men? The men seemed too scared to talk about anything.

Major Whitcombe seemed to think that General Colson was unaccountably insane, but there was no mystery as to what was wrong with Colson. The man was consumed by guilt. It had been obvious as soon as Fargo had put an end to all the women's palavering.

"I'm heading out to Minnesota," Fargo announced. "I heard about your daughter. I could look for her while I'm out there."

"Libby is dead," the general said flatly.

"Probably," Fargo agreed. "But the dead are best laid to rest, and that's kind of hard to do when somebody just disappears. If you'd give me a few particulars—what she looked like, where she was last seen, people she knew, what she had with her—I might be able to find something out."

The general was absolutely quiet, and the officers and their ladies held their breaths. Finally the general whispered. "I wouldn't know any of that. I haven't seen Libby since she was twelve years old."

Slowly, General Colson's story came out, related in such a way that it brought tears to the eyes of the ladies present, and none of them even liked Colson. As it turned out, the general's wife had died during the Mexican War. His young daughter had been sent to stay with his sister in Boston. Then came Comanche and Kiowa trouble, and Navaho and Apache trouble, and Cheyenne and Teton Sioux trouble, and finally a civil war. Altogether, General Colson had gotten around to seeing his daughter maybe four or five times, but not once in the past ten years.

General Colson was crazy all right; he was crazy with guilt. He kept wondering aloud whether he'd done the right thing in letting his Libby get married. His sister had opposed Elizabeth Colson's marrying at sixteen.

"My sister said the girl only wanted to marry because she was at an awkward age, and she felt gawky, big, and ungraceful. Thought nobody would ever ask her again." The general smiled wistfully and murmured, "Libby looked so much like her mother as a child. But I guess she turned out taking after me."

Colson seemed to feel guilty over that too, although Fargo couldn't imagine what a man was supposed to do about such a thing. Colson was lantern-jawed, hawk-beaked, and stood at least five inches over six feet tall.

Those attributes looked fine on him, but Fargo could sure see how they'd lead to depression in a sixteen-year-old girl.

"Libby's intended came all the way out to Fort Yuma, California, to see me," the general rambled on. "Frasier was an older man, over forty, a minister. He said he needed a wife in his profession. He genuinely seemed to admire my Libby. Said she was kind, intelligent, honest, well brought up. He wasn't the kind of man who would care that she was ungainly on the dance floor, which I gather she was from her letters. Libby was always worrying because she was taller than the boys, fretting that she was clumsy, that she was hopeless. I thought Frasier would take care of her."

Fargo didn't have the heart to remind Colson that Frasier had been dead three years. Dead men didn't take very good care of women.

Colson just kept mumbling, "I knew the West. I knew better than to let her marry a man who was going West."

But what almost certainly bothered Colson more than Libby going West was that he had left her living alone for three years after her husband's death. Colson didn't mention it, but it showed a pretty big oversight. Colson hadn't gone to his daughter's wedding or her husband's funeral, and he hadn't visited the widow once in all that time.

But Libby had traveled to Boston to visit her aunt during those years. Knowing that made Fargo wonder if the general had ever even asked his daughter to visit him. Whether Colson had or not, he was paying for his neglect now. So were all the other people at Fort Laramie. Fargo had never been as happy to leave a place behind as he had been last week when he'd ridden his Ovaro away from the fort. Now he had a feeling he was going to be just as happy to get on his pinto and ride out of Nebraska.

Fargo hadn't meant to get Belle in trouble; she was an old friend. But the general probably hadn't meant to ignore his daughter, either. Those things just happened. And feeling bad about them didn't help any. Guilt only served to make people act as crazy as the general.

"Women," Fargo muttered into his whiskey.

Women. Who needed them? Who wanted them? As he picked up his tenth glass of whiskey, Fargo was almost glad there weren't any women working in the saloon that night.

"Hey, cowboy," a young farmer taunted. "We don't need your kind here."

Fargo turned to look at him. "Cowboy?" he blurted. "You mean me?"

"Yeah, you," the swaggering hayseed countered.

Fargo understood why farmers didn't like cowboys. Cows had a nasty habit of trampling over crops. And why cowboys didn't like farmers. Farmers were always plowing up good grazing land. But, hell, Nebraska was still damned near empty.

"I'm not a cowboy," Fargo chafed.

"You farm?" the young ruffian demanded.

"Hell, no," Fargo spat decisively.

"Then you ain't welcome here," the man announced, reaching out to tip over Fargo's drink.

Fargo figured he'd been leaning too heavily on the bar or the young sodbuster never would have accosted him. Grinning, Fargo straightened, drew his arm back, and sent the intruder flying backward. Feeling better than he had all evening, Fargo watched the man land in the middle of a poker game.

Grabbing the young farmer by the collar, one of the gawking cardplayers pulled him up off the table and sent him sprawling across the floor. "What you do that for?" he shouted at Fargo. "I was winning."

"I was just evening up the odds," Fargo laughed.

"It wasn't funny," the card player protested, stalking up to the Trailsman.

Fargo didn't quit laughing, but he dodged the man's swing. Recovering his balance, Fargo slammed his fist into the man's gut. The man was big and stocky. He staggered, but he didn't fall.

"Wait, let me have him," one of the other cardplayers begged, swinging at the stocky man's jaw. "He wasn't winning. He was cheating."

The newcomer to the fight was so drunk his swing missed entirely. His follow-through, however, sent him careening into his staggering poker partner, and both of them went down. The two cardplayers sprawled on the floor, the one on top passed-out drunk, the one underneath heaving for air. The farmer was still flat on his back, moaning and rubbing the back of his head where it had bounced on the wooden floor.

All three of them stayed down. Several men gathered to see what was happening, but none seemed interested in continuing the fracas.

"Shit," Fargo muttered as he left the saloon. "A man can't even get in a good fight hereabouts."

The next morning, it took Fargo several minutes to realize that the persistent throbbing wasn't only in his head. The awful pounding was at the door. "Go away," he shouted as he tried to squint through the onslaught of sunshine pouring through his hotel room window.

"Skye?" Belle called. "Please?"

Grimacing, Fargo got up and answered the door. "What do you want?" he demanded more gruffly than he meant to.

Cowering a little, Belle gazed down at Fargo's naked pelvis. "Oh," he laughed.

Knowing from her startled look that *he* wasn't what she wanted that morning, Fargo sauntered over and pulled his pants on. When he turned around, Belle was inside his room, leaning on the closed door. Belle's dark-blue calico dress was plain, but her figure more than made up for any lack of ornamentation. Her hair was pulled back to look neat and proper, but little wispy curls tickled her cheeks and forehead.

Fargo sprawled back down on the bed, leaning against the headboard and wishing he had a cup of coffee. "So what did you have in mind?" he asked.

"Please, Skye. You got to help me with Tommy."

"Help you? Seems to me you get in enough trouble with men all by yourself, Belle."

"Oh, Skye. He means to get hisself killed," she cried. "He told me them soldiers at Laramie want him and he plans on turning hisself in."

"Now?" Fargo blurted.

"No, he's got writing to finish up. Next October, I guess. But you can't let him do it, Skye. He ain't done nothing but wrote and talked. That ain't illegal, is it?"

"There's a general who thinks it is," Fargo replied. "And he thinks Bradford's done a few things too, like selling whiskey and guns to the Indians."

Belle blanched. "Please, Skye. Take me to Laramie. I'll tell them he ain't done nothing." She shook her head back and forth, and the light glistened in the pale curls framing her face. "I swear he didn't do nothing like that, not in all the time I knowed him." Belle stepped forward and perched on the edge of the bed, carefully sitting a foot away from Fargo's long, lean legs. "I'll pay you," she offered, scrambling with the laces of her little crocheted handbag.

"Put your money away, Belle. I'm not going to take you to Laramie." Fargo paused. "But I'll take care of Bradford," he admitted reluctantly. Whitcombe was already paying him to do just that, but Fargo wasn't at all sure it was the best thing to do for Belle.

She squealed and launched herself at his chest. "Really?" she cried, throwing her arms around him.

"I guess so," he affirmed, feeling her sigh of relief as her magnificent bosom heaved against his chest. Belle buried her face against his shoulder and gave in to pent-up tears.

"It's all right," Fargo murmured. "I'll see he doesn't get to Fort Laramie."

"Thank you," she sniffled. "Oh, Skye, thank you. I just didn't know what to do." Leaning her head back, she summoned her best smile, the one that had made her the most popular woman in San Francisco.

Fargo put his hands on Belle's shoulders and firmly pushed her an arm's length away. He supposed he loved her a little, certainly not like a sister but not exactly like an ordinary lover either. Belle was an old friend. Drifting the way he did, Fargo didn't have all that many friends and over the years Belle DeVista had proved to be one of the best and the truest.

"I suspect Tommy wouldn't like your being here," he muttered.

"Oh," Belle gasped, stiffening. "Oh, Skye, I'm sorry. I shouldn't have . . . You know I can't . . ." she protested, staring at his bare chest in horror.

Fargo was beginning to feel a little chastened by the way Belle kept innocently flying into his arms as if he were a priest. "I didn't figure you could." He shrugged. "The way I remember it, you were always loyal. I guess I can't fault that. I just hope Tommy appreciates it."

Belle nodded and the door flew open.

"Goddamn," Fargo grumbled. "Speak of the devil."

At least Belle wasn't in his arms anymore, but Fargo figured Thomas Bradford was going to take enough exception to her sitting on his bed. For a single moment everyone was silent as Belle gaped and Bradford scowled.

"What is the meaning of this?" Bradford finally thundered.

"No meaning," Fargo explained hastily. "Belle was worried about you. She wanted to know about the charges against you. That's all."

"And you expect me to believe that? A man finds his wife in another man's hotel room sitting on his bed when that man is half-naked and . . ."

"His wife?" Fargo burst in.

"Oh. I assume she didn't tell you, then. Did she also neglect to inform you that she was no longer practicing her former profession? Or perhaps that was my false assumption. Perhaps Annabelle is here to earn her keep. Well, Annabelle, which is it? Are you in his bed because he's an old friend? Or because you wanted the money? God knows, I warned you that I was not a wealthy man."

"Oh, Tommy, you can't believe that. You just can't," Belle whispered.

"God damn it, Annabelle," Bradford blasted. "I loved you. I loved you and look what you've done to me."

Bradford stood in the doorway clenching his fists, his face red with fury. "Do you know what the Indians do with adulterous women?" he asked harshly, glaring at Belle. "They cut off their noses, slash off their hair, gash their cheeks. Sometimes they kill them. You should be grateful, Annabelle, that in spite of my beliefs I am still merely a poet."

Bradford's gaze shifted to Fargo. Hatred molded the contours of the poet's face, making the young man look older. For a second Fargo thought Bradford was going to challenge him, but then he stomped out, slamming the door so hard a mirror bounced off the wall and shattered.

Colored beams of light played off the silvered glass, dappling bright splotches on the dully papered walls.

"Belle, are you really married to him?" Fargo finally asked.

Belle stared at the broken pieces of mirror, nodding dazedly.

"Shit," Fargo cursed. "I was hoping he was just a temporary affliction."

"I have to go to him," Belle whispered.

"Belle, not now. Give him some time to calm down."

"I can't," she told Fargo. But Belle was dry-eyed now. Moving slowly but resolutely, with her head held high, her shoulders straight and her tiny frame rigidly erect, Belle rose and walked out the door, looking for all the world as if she were going to her own execution.

Fargo spent most of the day checking out the town. For the frontier, it was substantial, boasting not only the four-story hotel but a solid brick bank building. Someday most of Nebraska was bound to look pretty substantial, if only because there wasn't enough wood to build the flimsy shacks that graced the new Colorado mining camps. And though it was pretty dry by some standards, Nebraska was nonetheless too damp and cold for the adobe shanties that sprouted in the Southwest.

That evening, Fargo treated himself to a good steak and retired to his favorite saloon to muse on his plans for leaving on the morrow. He and the Ovaro had had enough rest, and the town, substantial as it was, wasn't big enough for more than a day's diversion. He was on his way back from the saloon when Belle found him.

"Skye," she called from the dark alleyway between the hotel and the haberdashery.

"Belle? Are you all right?"

"I'm all right," she answered in a muffled voice.

"He kicked you out," Fargo concluded.

"Uh huh," she agreed.

"Why did you come here?"

"I don't have any money."

Fargo sighed. Belle had made no attempt to come out of the shadows so Fargo plunged into the black alley, took her hand, and led her out. "I guess I'll have to sneak you in," he told her. "Since you're still a married woman."

Belle followed placidly, not speaking.

"Bradford won't like it if he finds out you came here," Fargo warned her, pushing Belle in front of him to tackle the metal fire-escape ladder.

The ladder was difficult to negotiate in the dark, and it had to be doubly difficult with skirts on. Fargo kept one hand firmly planted on Belle's bottom, not trusting her to pay attention to what she was doing.

"It don't matter no more," she told Fargo hollowly. "Tommy told me I wasn't good for him anyway. Told me I'd ruined his life. Said I took his mind off important things. Said I made him forget what was revelant."

"Relevant," Fargo corrected automatically. "Belle, do you think you can climb in that window?"

Belle didn't answer, she merely did what was suggested, hiking her calico skirts up around her thighs to swing her legs over the ledge. The window Fargo had chosen opened onto the second-floor hallway. The corridor had a wall lantern at the stairway end, but otherwise it was dark and shadowy. With a hand on her back, Fargo urged Belle toward the stairway.

"Said he'd started to hate me long ago. Said I destroyed him."

"Aw, Belle. That was just his anger talking. Why don't you wait a few days and see what happens?"

"No," she refused. "Tommy said I was a whore. Said he used to think that didn't matter. Said he'd never realized before that whoring wasn't something a woman did—it was something she was. He told me most women didn't take no pleasure in sex, but them that does, they's whores. And it ain't right tying them down 'cause they's meant by nature to be promiscus."

"Promiscuous," Fargo amended, realizing how slowly she was talking. "Belle, have you been drinking?"

"A little," she confessed. "Tommy told me he was sorry. Told me whores was a thing of nature. Whores ain't bad or nothing, but they prompt men toward violence. Said he never wanted to see me again. Said it was wrong, me trying to be with one man. It was against the unity stuff he talks about."

"That's all bullshit," Fargo snapped, stopping in front of his room on the third floor. He fumbled the key into the lock in spite of the poor light.

"I don't know," she sighed. "I never did understand Tommy too good. But I loved him. I did," she sniffed defensively, as if Fargo was going to argue with her.

"I'm sure you did," Fargo said as he stepped into his room. "Bradford was your type of man."

"You really think so?" Belle asked, brightening a little. "Then you don't think it was wrong, me loving him? Tommy was so smart. Read me poetry and stuff—never even had trouble with them big words. He knew what they meant and everything." She sighed. "But I guess I always knew he wouldn't stay with a woman like me."

"Here, let me get the lantern lit," Fargo offered. "Goddamn," he swore as he turned back toward the door. "The son of a bitch hit you."

"It was only a little slap," she objected.

"It sure as hell wasn't a love pat," Fargo groused, stepping up to Belle to turn her cheek toward the light. Her jawline was dark purple and puffy.

"It wasn't his fault," she protested, jerking her chin from Fargo's grasp and flouncing away. Glaring at Fargo defiantly, Belle sat down.

"It wasn't his fault," Fargo mocked. "I suppose you just happened to step in front of Bradford's fist?"

The chair Belle sat in was huddled in the corner, sharing the little nightstand with the bed, but Fargo had placed the lantern on the dresser behind him. Its rays illuminated only the determined jut of Belle's jaw. Her bruise was lost in the shadows.

"I got mad," she explained. "I yelled some, broke near every dish in the place. Then I tried to hit him with

the frying pan. 'Cept I missed. It wasn't right, but . . .''
Belle's chin quivered, but she raised her head insolently
and her eyes sparkled dangerously. "He promised," she
finished sharply.

Fargo had known Belle for years, but he'd never seen
her mad enough to break anything. "What did he promise?" Fargo asked.

For several moments Belle stared at Fargo. Finally she
bowed her head and the light glowed softly on her yellow
hair. "He promised it didn't matter," she whispered.
"Said he didn't care what I'd been."

"Aw, shit," Fargo spat. "Belle, haven't you heard
enough promises in your life to know better?"

"Tommy's different," she insisted.

"Different? You can say that again. Tommy's crazier
than any dozen asylum inmates."

Belle's head jerked up. "He ain't crazy," she shouted
stubbornly.

"You've heard him," Fargo persisted. "Belle, you
were born out West. Do you really think all the farmers,
ranchers, miners, shopkeepers, and soldiers are just going to up and go east? Then when the Indians want the
East back everybody is just going to take sail, right?"
he scoffed. Fargo sat down on the edge of the bed facing
Belle, and his voice grew more cajoling. "Come on,
Belle. What with the smallpox and the measles there
probably aren't more than a couple hundred thousand Indians left in this whole country. Never were that many—
Indians don't have a tendency to overpopulate. But I
reckon there are more than a couple of million white
people in an average state like Ohio. What chance do the
Indians really have? You don't really believe Bradford's
plan can work, do you?"

"No," she whispered. "But that doesn't matter," she
added. Raising her head, Belle looked very small and
glum. Fargo was sitting close enough to see the way the
swelling distorted her jawline, and he knew from experience that a bruise like that hurt whenever you so much
as moved your head. Normally Belle smiled away her
problems, pretending they didn't exist, like she had over

DeLacey. Maybe it was the ache in her jaw that was getting to her.

"I'm going to go deck that asshole," Fargo announced abruptly, standing up.

"No," Belle objected. "Please don't. You got to understand. You got to try to understand," she begged.

"Why?" Fargo blasted.

" 'Cause Tommy ain't an asshole," she denied. "He ain't stupid, neither. He knows his dreams probably can't work, but he's got to try. Tommy says men need a place to escape to. Says they need a frontier. A place for dreaming and adventuring. It's always been that way, even as far back as that odd sea story of Homer's. But the men coming out here, they bring farms and towns and all that stuff. Tommy says soon there won't be noplace different left. You can see that, can't you, Skye? How white men make everything the same?"

"Dammit, Belle. Sure, I can see some of Bradford's point. But he's crazy. He can't change the world."

"No," she murmured. "But he's got to try. A man's got to try to do what he thinks is right, don't he?"

"Goddamn it. What difference does it make?" Fargo demanded impatiently. "Bradford's plan is crazy."

"Goddamn it, don't you understand nothing, Skye Fargo? Maybe I don't understand much. And I'll admit I don't even know half them fancy words Tommy uses. But I know he's got some good ideas. And he's got the right to spread 'em. You and me and the army—none of us got the right to stop him."

Belle looked as harmless as an annoyed kitten, but her eyes gleamed with all the fury of an enraged mountain lion. Fargo had never seen Belle so angry. He gaped at her. "Settle down, Belle."

"Settle down, calm down, cool off. You and Tommy are just full of advice today, ain't you?"

"Shit," Fargo huffed. "What did I do?"

"You ain't done nothing," Belle bristled. "You know when I was a little girl we had a neighbor lady. Her husband died of the cholera and she was left with fourteen children. And nobody did nothing, 'cept my ma. There's rich folks and there's poor folks. My folks was always poor, but my ma gave that widow lady food just the same. Until my pa put a stop to it.''

Pausing to catch her breath, Belle scowled at Fargo, practically daring him to interrupt her. Although he was finding it easier by the minute to see how Bradford's fist might have been provoked, Fargo was too fascinated at seeing this new side to Belle to really even want to stop her. Who would have believed that sweet, meek little Belle would try to brain a man with a frying pan?

"My pa said we didn't have nothing and we couldn't afford to give nothing,'' Belle continued indignantly. "But the richer folks, they never did give nothing. They thought the poor deserved what they got. What with the way they lived and all—you know, poor and without nothing. Seemed to think the poor didn't care about nothing worthwhile,'' she stormed. "Didn't seem to notice the poor didn't *have* nothing worthwhile. They all just left that widow lady with fourteen hungry, whining children. And do you know what that widow lady did?'' Belle demanded. "She took all them children out to the barn and shot 'em. Later she said bullets was cheaper than bread.''

Fargo winced. "Jesus Christ, Belle. That's the most disgusting story I've ever heard.''

"But it's true,'' she fumed.

"I'm sure it is. But what's it got to do with anything?''

Belle stared at him and her anger faded away until she merely looked puzzled. She looked confused and hurt, and Fargo figured she'd had way too much to drink. He felt sorry for her, but he wasn't about to chance igniting another tantrum.

"What's it got to do with anything?'' she mumbled. "Everything,'' she answered immediately. "Don't you see, Skye? Tommy's got to do what he can. Maybe he can't do much. But he's got to try. Everybody's got to keep trying,'' she pleaded. "Sometimes it can make a difference. After all, who would have thought my ma with her bread and vegetable scraps could have made a difference to that widow lady? But she did.''

"And just what do you think Tommy can do?'' Fargo asked quietly.

"I don't know," Belle answered. "Probably nothing, here. And now. But maybe someday folks won't be so anxious to change every place they come to. Maybe they'll read Tommy's stuff. And maybe they'll think twice about the way they live—the way Tommy wants 'em to. And someday, maybe it'll be an island Tommy saves. Or maybe part of Africa. But the idea that when folks come from somewhere else they should learn to live like the folks that's already there, that makes sense. Leastways it does to me."

Belle lapsed into silence. Somehow, even with all her convoluted reasoning, she had given Fargo far more appreciation for Bradford's crazy ideals than Bradford had managed to instill. Perhaps Belle should have been the one giving his speeches.

"Belle, why don't you try getting some sleep?" Fargo suggested. "I'll lay my bedroll out on the floor and you can have the bed. Tomorrow morning, we'll see what we can do about Bradford. I guess you care for him more than I figured."

"I love him," she murmured. "But it's over. Tommy says I make him fall into all the things he believes is wrong. Living in a cabin, making curtains, planting a garden. Ruining the land forever."

"There's nothing wrong with the things you do, Belle."

"I don't know," she murmured tiredly. "What's good? What's bad? What's right? What's wrong? Sometimes I just can't think on those things. It gives me a headache."

Sighing wearily, Belle stood up and started unbuttoning the front of her calico gown while Fargo tactfully turned away. "Skye, would you sleep with me tonight?" she asked abruptly.

Fargo spun around but wished he hadn't. The corset she wore only served to squeeze her soft white skin into awesomely swelling curves, and the tops of her breasts surged right out of her unbuttoned gown. Belle dropped her dress to the floor and turned around, waving to indicate the hooks on the back of her corset.

"Belle, are you sure?" he asked. For friendship's sake, he had to ask, but as his fingers swiftly dealt with Belle's

46

hooks he wasn't entirely positive he'd let her change her mind, even if she wanted to.

"I reckon I've paid plenty for being a whore," she answered. "I should get something out of it, don't you think?" Belle twisted, leaning her head back to smile up at him. "And you, Skye Fargo, are as good as any woman ever gets."

4

Belle was a tiny thing, not even five feet tall, small but plump in all the right places. Only her breasts were out of proportion. Fargo cupped them in his hands, marveling as he always had that nature could get so confused in endowing this little woman with a bosom that would be considered outsized on a fat, matronly mother of a dozen children.

For all her colorful past, Belle was only twenty. Her face was young, her eyes round, her hair soft and glowing. Fargo's thumbs circled the erect nipples of breasts that were higher and firmer than they had any right to be. And Belle gazed up at him with an expression that looked more innocent and trusting than it had any call to look.

The swelling of her jaw had worsened, spreading a vivid bruise across her cheek, much darker than her ivory skin and nearly as blue as her glittering gaze. "Shit," Fargo muttered, realizing immediately that it wasn't the most romantic thing to say.

Belle's chin quivered, but she smiled as she loosened his belt buckle. "I'll make it good," she promised, pushing his clothing down. Belle sank to her knees and her tongue darted out to tease Fargo's erect organ.

Belle was not only a professional, she had an instinctual feel for what pleased a man. Her tongue flicked hotly while her fingers alternately stroked and squeezed, finding just the right rhythm.

Fargo was building up too fast. He could feel the pounding in his bloodstream. Automatically he glanced around, looking for a wall to lean on. Instead of finding one, he lifted Belle up and carried her to the bed.

Trying to catch his breath, Fargo embraced her. With

one hand buried in her silken hair, he used the other to smooth her lush curves. But Belle wiggled lose. Before he knew what she was up to, her full breasts and belly oozed down against his hard muscles and she clamped her lips back onto his throbbing shaft in earnest.

Skye Fargo seldom had any trouble with women—except Belle. He liked women, they liked him, and everything always seemed to work out all right in the end. But Belle had this knack for making him feel bad. Fargo had never run into a woman who could make his body feel better or his conscience feel worse. And there was something about her this time that made him feel even worse than usual.

There was almost a desperation in her eagerness. Besides that, her jaw had to be aching like the dickens. She was going much too fast, and she was trembling and nervous. Belle had had a bad day, and she deserved to be shown a little caring.

Not that Belle made that easy. It took all Fargo's will just to keep from grinding his pelvis against her bruised jaw. It was time she found out he could be considerate, maybe even gentle.

Belle's mouth worked urgently. It was compelling, but it wasn't what Fargo had in mind. "Belle," he gasped. "Slow down."

Belle raised her head. "You don't like it?" she asked dazedly. "I'm sorry," she whispered. "I guess I can try something else."

Her head dropped back down again. Fargo jerked and his breath caught in his throat. He had no idea what she'd done, but for a second he thought he'd lost all opportunity to show her anything, at least for another twenty minutes or so. But then the world righted itself and he realized he was still in the running.

Fargo reached down and touched her hair. "Belle, your jaw has got to hurt already. Why don't you come up here? It'll be warm. It'll be nice," he coaxed.

Belle lifted her head and stared at him. "But I want to do something for you," she protested.

"Aw, Belle," he complained, "you always want to do something for everyone."

"You sound just like Tommy," she whimpered. "I don't do this for just everybody. Leastways not unless I got to, and I don't got to do it for you."

"Belle, maybe what you need to do is talk. Why don't you tell me what's wrong?"

"Haven't you heard? Everything's wrong with me."

"Come on, Belle," Fargo moaned. "Why don't you come up here and put your arms around me. We've never fought before."

"No, we haven't. But that's 'cause it takes two to fight, and you're always telling me what to do. I never get a word in edgewise."

"Jesus," Fargo groaned. He had always thought Belle should quit being so damned obliging, but she had sure picked a hell of a time to become argumentative. Why couldn't she have waited until he was out of Nebraska? Then, if she still felt like it, she could gun down everybody in the territory for all he cared.

Considering that it was Bradford who had walked out on her, Fargo didn't figure he should have to put up with Belle's temper. But she still clutched his erect organ in her fist. This wasn't his fight; this was Bradford's fight, and the rational part of Fargo wished she would just leave him out of it. But that wasn't the part Belle grasped in her hand.

"Look," he ground out with enormous effort. "You're obviously not in the mood for this. Why don't you give it up and try to get some sleep?"

"You're always telling me what to do," Belle exploded, tossing her head back and glaring at him. Her eyes flashed with lightning in the moonlit room. "You don't seem to think I'm smart enough to decide anything for myself. Well, I'll show you, Skye Fargo. I ain't some stupid little ninny. There's things I know. I can take care of myself."

"I give up," Fargo chafed. "I don't care. Do whatever you want, Belle."

With a defiant gesture Belle flipped her long hair behind her shoulder before she dipped her head down again. And Fargo lay back against the pillows, obstinately determined to ignore her.

Her breath was hot on his flesh. Her tongue swirled and twisted. Her mouth nibbled. Fargo took a deep breath and folded his arms across his chest.

With her breasts pressed against his thighs and her legs wrapped around his knees, Belle drew him in farther than he thought possible. There were definitely things Belle knew. There were things her mouth knew, and things her tongue knew. Within seconds Fargo wasn't sure he knew anything at all. He summoned his stoicism, but it didn't come. His hands flew to his sides, gripping the bed covers with white-knuckled intensity. And Belle drew him in even farther, suckling with all the avid eagerness of a hungry calf.

"Shit, what am I fighting for?" Fargo rasped, momentarily relaxing, only to find himself twisting sideways.

He grasped Belle's bare shoulders and thrust forward blindly, but she didn't falter. She was pulling him apart. It felt as if his guts were being drawn out. Her slender arms clasped him closer, and her legs twined around his. She was all wrapped up with him, squeezing him like a boa constrictor and moving with him as he thrust.

All thought of control was gone. Fargo didn't give a damn anymore that Belle not only had a sore jaw but was upset and maybe more than a little drunk. He surged into her mindlessly, but Belle didn't let up.

She was greedy. She shifted to one side, leaning her head back while her fingers clawed his buttocks, forcing him forward while her mouth worked frantically, urging him on.

There was nothing gentle about it. Belle shifted again, Fargo lunged. The bed covers slipped off one side of the bed. The pillows flew in the opposite direction. Fargo clutched Belle's hair, and she slammed her pelvis against his leg, tugging at him with her mouth until the pounding swept through him, throbbing in his ears and hammering at his chest.

He ignited like black powder. And blew like nitro.

But relief was sweet. There was forgetfulness and oblivion cloaking him in their hazy void. His body pulsed lazily. He drifted. He floated.

Fargo didn't notice anything at all until he realized he

was cold. His sweat was drying on his skin. And beside him, Belle was curled into a little, shivering ball. Fargo got up to retrieve the pillows and blankets, and for a moment the room spun crazily. Belle had a way of not letting any blood get to a man's brain. Laughing, Fargo spread the blankets out on the bed before he climbed back in and pulled Belle close.

"Are you all right?" he asked, trying to warm her chilled skin.

Belle merely nodded, her head rubbing against his chest.

"For such a little thing, you sure do pack a wallop," he teased her.

"I'm sorry about how I've been," she whispered. "I didn't mean to lay my troubles on you."

"It's all right, Belle."

"No, it ain't," she sniffed. "You're a good man, Skye Fargo. You don't lie to women. And you don't never make promises you can't keep. You shouldn't have to pay for them that do. I don't know what got into me," she murmured apologetically. "I wasn't very nice."

"Don't be silly, Belle. I thought you were nice."

She was quiet, too quiet. The breasts pressed against his chest were still, and the warm breath on his shoulder was halting. She was obviously struggling to hold back tears.

"But on the other hand," Fargo bantered, "if this is what a woman thinks is mean, I guess I'll just have to convince all of them that I meet from here on out that I'm the enemy."

He had hoped she would laugh, just a little. Or at least smile. Belle had always been good about smiling, even when she didn't feel like it. But she wasn't this time. With one arm wrapped around his neck, she pressed herself against Fargo, seeming to cling more than snuggle. And he could feel the quiver in her jaw.

"Belle, would you like to talk?" he asked.

"No," she answered.

Which was probably just as well. He'd done his part, and it had left him feeling pleasantly tired. Fargo tugged up the covers and settled in. But the hazy drifting had left him, and sleep didn't come.

"What are you going to do about your marriage?" he asked finally.

"Nothing," she whispered.

"You going to stay around here?"

"For a while. I've got some things to take care of."

"Then you'll be seeing Bradford again?"

"No," she denied. "Well, I mean . . . It's a small town. I guess I'll see him. But he ain't what I got to take care of." Belle sighed and leaned her head back to look at Fargo. Her eyes glistened unnaturally in the dim room. "Skye, do you think I could borrow a hundred dollars from you?"

"Sure. I can spare a hundred. I reckon I owe you that. And more."

"No," she refused. "I ain't just taking it. I'll pay you back. With interest. Like with a bank."

"We're friends," Fargo bristled. "Money doesn't matter."

"No," Belle retorted. "Friends ain't the same when there's money. Things ain't the same with money."

"Goddamn it," Fargo cursed, losing his patience. "You won't let me do anything for you. You never would let me do anything for you."

"That ain't true, Skye. You've done plenty for me."

"Like what? Fucked you," he taunted. "Sure, I've done that on several occasions. And tomorrow I've got to leave for Minnesota. I'll be leaving you here, in a godforsaken town with a man who's half mad when he's in the best of moods. And he'll sure be angry if he finds out about tonight. Where are your clothes, Belle? He's got your clothes. He's got your things. And you're his wife. Do you know what that means? It means nobody's going to lift a finger if he hurts you."

"Tommy wouldn't hurt me.'

"He wouldn't?" Fargo scoffed, tilting her chin back. He saw the damp tear tracks on her cheeks as he glared at her swollen jaw. "He'd hurt you," Fargo assured her fervently. "And you know the funny thing? I can't even blame him. If you were my wife I just might kill you.

What Bradford did doesn't matter. Husbands don't have a tendency to stop and meditate on whether they deserved what they got.''

"Skye, you shouldn't worry so much," she pleaded. "Tommy and me was married in an Arapaho village. Weren't much to it," she mused solemnly. "They put up a tent, gave us some presents, then everybody came in and ate. And we was married. Tommy said it meant more to him that way. Maybe that was true. But I suspect the marriage ain't legal.''

"And you've been letting Bradford play Mr. Holier-than-thou because he dragged you through a tepee?" Fargo snapped. "What kind of a marriage is that? There isn't a woman in this town that would think your kind of marriage was any better than being a whore. And that includes the whores. For God's sake, Belle, how do you get yourself into these fixes?''

"I ain't in no fix," she cried, but then she burst into tears.

"I'm sorry," Fargo mumbled. "I'm sorry," he repeated pulling her closer.

But he just didn't seem to be able to keep his mouth shut around Belle. He was always preaching at her. He was worse than Bradford. Fargo clamped his mouth down over Belle's lips more because he didn't want to start ranting at her again than because he wanted to kiss her.

But Belle responded. She trembled all over. Her arms shook and her breasts jiggled against his chest. Fargo didn't rightly know whether she wanted him or if she was just fixing to cry some more.

But he wanted her. He kissed her cheeks, her neck, her collarbone. He buried his face against her billowing breasts, suckled on the hard nipples, and pressed his lips to her soft belly.

Belle was too overwrought to flare up like she usually did. She just kept running her fingers through his hair until her hips began to undulate with need. She moaned and Fargo moved back up and entered her.

Belle clutched Fargo tightly in her arms and wrapped her legs around him as she swept up to receive him. She took him deep into her moist center, and her muscles strained to hold him there.

She gasped as he pulled back, then immediately slammed her pelvis back against him. "No," she cried as he withdrew. Her hips soared up and crushed into his. "No," she repeated, seemingly intent on keeping all of him inside of her. Fargo pulled back again, and her hands flew down. With her palms pressing into his backside, Belle tried to force him back in.

His laughter flowed, suddenly and easily, as he teased her, retreating once again. Belle surged up, impaling herself on his erect organ. Her pelvis ground into his. Her hips gyrated. And Fargo edged back, eluding her, taunting her, making her work to have him.

"No, don't," she cried. "Please give it to me. Please." She jerked and rocked and twisted under him. "No," she whimpered, renewing her efforts. Belle's body sprang up and her thighs clamped down. "No," she whispered over and over until he couldn't resist any more. His thrusts answered the words.

"No, no, no, no, no," Belle breathed, plunging against Fargo so hard her pelvis seemed to fuse with his. Her body shook and her hot core shuddered, closing in on him.

Fargo struggled away one last time, grasping her hips in his hands and pinning her down with his weight, while Belle screeched wildly, fighting to hurl herself up against him. Her legs flailed. Her feet hit the bed. And the thighs squeezed in on him like the teeth of a trap as she threw her head back, clenched her teeth, and strained toward his groin.

But Fargo held himself aloof. He was winded and taut. His breath came fast, and the sweat poured off of him. His arms ached with the tension of holding her in place, but her greed filled him with heat.

"Please," Belle begged. Her thighs fell open and she spread her legs farther apart, arching her pelvis to reach out to him.

Fargo raised himself onto his elbows and stared at her large breasts. They glistened with sweat and heaved with exertion. He was poised at her portal, his shaft barely penetrating her dark recesses, but he felt her tension building.

Her need throbbed, wet and hot. Fargo lunged but feinted, once, twice, three times. Her muscles grabbed for him, awed him. Tortured him.

Belle groaned and the sound grew harsh and pained, as shrill with sex, urgency, and anger as the caterwauling of a cat. And Fargo rammed into her, flooding her with his seed.

They were wet. Her breasts were sticky, her belly slick. Fargo shifted his weight but made no attempt to leave her. Belle's hair was a tangled mess. Long, thick strands of it were soaked and plastered between them. The air was pungent with musk and perspiration and the sheets were damp, but their stink amused Fargo.

Idly stroking Belle's breast, he reveled at the whole vulgar, smelly nature of lovemaking. Pleased with the woman and the sex, he was well satisfied and content. His mind wandered far away from problems and serious thoughts.

"I love you," Belle whispered.

Fargo froze, and his hand fell from her breast. It didn't mean anything, he told himself. Women were always saying that. But Belle never had.

"But you love Bradford," he objected.

"I love him too," she admitted. "Tommy needed me," she told Fargo. "Tommy might be real smart, but he can barely feed himself without help. I like men who need me," she sighed. "You don't need nobody. But I love you just the same." Belle turned in Fargo's arms, reaching out to caress his bearded jaw. "I just wanted you to know in case . . . In case . . . If . . . I mean because . . ." She faltered, and her chin quivered.

"Belle, what do you expect to happen?" Fargo demanded.

"Nothing, Skye. Nothing at all. It ain't like that. I just wanted to tell you I loved you when you wasn't mad at me. I know what I am," she confessed meekly. "I know I do things that disgust you. And sometimes I just get scared that I'll do something really awful, really stupid.

56

I'm going to be all right, Skye. Really, I am. I just ain't so sure you'll always want to see me."

"What kind of way is that to talk?" he bristled. "Belle, we've known each other for six years. Have I ever avoided seeing you?"

"Please, Skye. I don't want to fight," Belle warned.

But he could tell by the way she fluttered her fingers across his mouth that she didn't agree with him, that she would have answered yes to his question. It was true. He had avoided her on a few occasions. But he wasn't disgusted with her; he was worried about her. If there was one thing in life a man could count on, though, it was that a woman would always jump to the worst conclusions.

"Belle, I'm sorry I blundered into your life," Fargo conceded gruffly. "And I'm sorry I messed things up with Bradford, but—"

"No," she broke in. "I said I loved you. I don't want you to say nothing. I don't expect you to do nothing. I just wanted you to know."

"Belle, you don't have to stay here. I could take you to Sioux City," he offered.

"No," she refused. "I'll be fine. You don't need to feel bad, Skye. I'm glad you came." She took a deep breath. "Skye," she said hesitantly. "You won't let Tommy get hisself killed, will you?"

"Oh, hell," Fargo growled. "No, I suppose not. Although it isn't as if the bastard deserves saving."

Belle smiled tremulously and her chin barely quivered, or at least Fargo couldn't see her well enough in the darkened room to notice its quivering.

"Skye," Belle chastened mildly as she turned around and snuggled back against him. "You've got riding to do in the morning. You'd best get some sleep. Besides, there ain't nothing for you to fret about. I reckon, considering what happened, that things never would have worked between me and Tommy anyway."

But sleep didn't come easily. Belle's manner bothered him. Her declaration of love, her bursts of temper, her edginess, her sentimentality, all told him more than her words. Something was wrong. There was something Belle wasn't telling him. Abruptly, and with certainty, Fargo knew it. Unfortunately, he didn't know how to pry it out of her without getting rough.

"Belle," Fargo ventured, realizing from the tense set of the shoulder blades nestling against his chest that she wasn't asleep. "What is it you're not telling me?"

Belle sighed wearily. "Nothing important," she whispered. "There's just some things a woman can't discuss with a man. Personal things, female things, the way she feels about herself. Them things ain't in a man's province. If I told you my worries you'd be real practical. But I don't want practical. I want to figure out for myself how I feel about things."

"Why don't you come with me?" Fargo invited. "I might have to leave you at Fort Ridgely for a while, but we could be together sometimes. We'd have a good time."

"Oh, Skye, you know you don't want to take me."

"That's not true," he denied.

"It is true," she countered. "And I won't go. Please, Skye, just leave it be."

"I could take you to Sioux City," he suggested. "We could spend a couple of days there. And then you could take the stage back to Lil's."

"Damm it, Skye Fargo," Belle blurted. "I don't want to go to Lil's. That's my problem—I can't just go running back to Lil's. Not this time. I got decisions to make and I got to make 'em myself. And it ain't your business so you just stay out of it, you hear?"

"I hear," Fargo snapped irritably. "But if you need anything you're going to wire me at Ridgely."

"Oh, Skye," Belle laughed. "That's why I love you. You're never around. But you're always there. I'll be fine," she assured him once again as she twisted around to kiss him on the lips.

But he couldn't seem to shake the terrible suspicion that Belle wasn't going to be fine. And that she already knew it.

5

Bradford couldn't have stunk more of whiskey if he had bathed in it. The air wafting through the door was eighty proof and smelled as if it could have been lit.

"What do you want?" The poet scowled at Fargo. Whereas only two days earlier the poet had looked like an eager adolescent, this morning his angry, unshaven visage would have scared small children. Bradford's eyes were bloodshot and red-rimmed, and his gaunt face was fiercely set beyond its dark shadow of day-old beard.

"To see you," Fargo answered easily. "I'm leaving for Minnesota, and I wanted to ask about your plans first."

"You can go to hell for all I care. And you can take Annabelle with you."

"Take it easy, Bradford. Belle just dropped by yesterday morning because she was worried about you. And that's the truth."

Fargo saw no reason to mention the evening. Belle was loyal, and she never would have come by if Bradford hadn't hurt her. As far as Fargo was concerned, if there was blame to be found the poet merely needed to look in the mirror. Regrettably, Fargo also knew there wasn't a chance in hell that Belle could be similarly circumspect. The woman was as compulsively self-destructive as she was loyal.

Fargo didn't like leaving Belle behind. There was hatred glinting in Bradford's red-eyed glare. The poet's soul gleamed in that gaze, and this morning it was ugly and twisted. Maybe Bradford really had loved Belle. Or maybe he had merely thought he owned her. Whichever it was, Bradford was in far worse shape than Fargo had expected him to be in.

"You really believe I'm a simpleton, don't you, Fargo?" Bradford hissed, and a muscle in his lean cheek twitched. "But I know what Annabelle is. She is a creature of nature, food for the male of our species, just as the mouse is food for the eagle, the hawk, and the coyote. Libidinous, hot, anxious to be devoured, shrieking her bestiality, she sates your hunger or mine. It makes no difference. But I am sickened by her tender flesh. And you are welcome to her."

"Belle decides that, not you," Fargo objected.

"Don't try to deceive me," Bradford roared. "I am no simpleton. A fool perhaps, as guilty as the pompous missionaries of trying to convert the carnal savage. But I know what Annabelle is. I know what she's done. I saw her enter your room last night. I heard her. I listened to her cries and ached as any man would upon hearing her lust. A panting, lewd, and covetous animal our Annabelle is. And yet I accept that it is her role to incite the rutting instinct. Or did you think she exhibited her heat only for you?"

Bradford attempted a knowing smile, but it turned into something more like a smirk. He pretended indifference poorly. His blurry-eyed glare was still intense and angry.

"Why, you sick bastard," Fargo exclaimed. "What did you do? Sit outside in the hall all night?"

"I didn't need to spend the night."

No. But Bradford must have lurked outside the door for several hours, most of it spent listening to nothing more than the sound of muffled conversation. And poor Belle had spent half that time defending this arrogant ignoramus. Fargo felt his temper surge. He didn't like the idea that this skinny pervert had gotten a rise out of listening at his hotel room door.

"You stupid, condescending, patronizing son of a bitch," Fargo spat. "You talk as if Belle was something other than human. Is that the way you feel about Indians too?"

"They are all what they were meant to be," Bradford intoned coldly. "They are no better and no worse."

"Well, I'll tell you something," Fargo snapped. "I've known Belle since she was fourteen years old, and there's nothing wrong with what she is. Belle does what she has to. And she gives some genuine caring with the sex. And that's goddamn rare.''

Bradford's feathers were ruffling and the hollow chest was puffing right up, getting ready to blast invective back at Fargo.

"But then Belle has always been a generous woman,'' Fargo announced quickly, before Bradford could get started again. "Once after a mine accident, she sent everything she had to the bereft families. Didn't hold back so much as a nickel. Made Lil so mad she kicked Belle out for a week—since there's not much glamour in running a high-toned place when your best girl is down to a patched, gray linsey-woolsey shift and torn cotton stockings.

"Poor Lil's one of the most astutely greedy business-women in the West, but Belle has forced her into being charitable time and time again. There was always too much profit for Lil in replacing Belle's wardrobe,'' Fargo reflected. "And nobody could ever stop Belle from giving it away again. Because, whether you admit it or not,'' Fargo finished with an edge in his voice, "Belle's a good woman.''

"Annabelle is my wife,'' Bradford stated grimly. His rigid body blocked the doorway and his words seethed out through clenched teeth, sounding hoarse and strained. "But in spite of that, I know exactly what she is. You needn't remind me that she performed the duties of her vocation in a brothel.''

"Shit,'' Fargo swore. "You don't hear a goddamned thing, do you? You've been so busy pouring all your feelings out onto clean, white pages that you're as empty and dry as a piece of parchment. Oh sure, you're mad, all right. I suspect you could burn right up like a piece of tinder. But there isn't any juice left in you. The truth is, Belle is too fucking good for you, Bradford. And she's damnably lucky I came along when I did.''

"I'm surprised you're not taking Belle with you,'' Bradford remarked sarcastically. "Assuming you really do feel the way you proclaim you do.''

"I'd take Belle with me in a minute,'' Fargo retorted, realizing instantaneously that he was speaking the truth.

To hell with Bradford. He should just marry Belle himself. Fargo knew from experience that Belle seldom complained about anything, not dust, not dirt, not heat, not cold, not other women. Belle wouldn't complain about living on the trail. She was the kind of woman who would cook, wash, sew, and take care of the horses. And she'd be glad to do it.

But then Fargo remembered her garden and her curtains. And he knew he couldn't give her those things. And he recalled how her chin quivered whenever he so much as raised his voice. And how she was always apologizing for nothing. And he knew for certain that he could never live with Belle.

"But Belle doesn't want to come with me," Fargo acknowledged finally, knowing it was for the best but feeling a kind of bittersweet loss at the knowledge.

"Perhaps you think I should be grateful that you came here to so kindly inform me that my wife displays the same fickle sentiments toward you that she has shown toward me," Bradford scoffed. "But tell me, Fargo. Does it bother you that it will be another man who tastes the salt between those wondrous breasts? Because in spite of what you term my empty, dry, and juiceless nature, it bothers me."

Bradford flexed his hand before grasping the door frame in a siege of anger. "Imagine it, Fargo. Imagine the man who has already come to take your place. He's there, right now, pressing his face to Annabelle's mound of Venus, dipping his tongue to taste her lust. He's lapping away the residue of your carnal pleasure, tasting your stale seed. He's rutting against Belle's breasts, smearing his juice onto her dusky nipples."

Fargo stared at Bradford. The man could condemn Belle for being a whore if he wanted to, but Bradford sure wasn't full of puritan ethics himself. Smelling like the inside of a whiskey barrel, the poet squinted irritably at the bright spring day. Then grimacing, he brought a hand up to rub his temple. From the look of Bradford, it was easy to conclude he was suffering from one hell of a hangover. His eyes matched his rumpled, red flannel shirt. And he was sweaty and trembling. After pausing only momentarily to ease his headache, Bradford launched into yet another obscene fantasy.

"He's a fat man," Bradford ranted on. "A mountain of doughy flesh. Annabelle is trying to make the man hurry because there are others waiting, for that is Annabelle's business, of course. She pleads and moans and begs for him. She whispers words she has used with you and with me to encourage him. But the man is clumsy and overeager. He labors awkwardly between her widespread thighs; his pink buttocks, fat and soft and dimpled, quivers as he lunges. He misses. His huge, flaccid belly lies between them. He drools on her soft white breast. He is panting. His face is red. He bobs ineffectively. While his hand fumbles at Annabelle's hot, wet nether lips, Annabelle tries to guide his swollen purple flesh inside."

Although Fargo couldn't imagine Belle with anyone this morning—since he knew damned well that she was back at the hotel crying her eyes out—Bradford obviously could imagine it. And he was doing a damned good job of it. Actually, Bradford was making Fargo feel a little queasy, and Fargo had thought he was immune to such indispositions.

Swallowing back nausea, Fargo found himself awed that Bradford's tirade could affect him so. "Jesus Christ," Fargo groaned in distaste as the poet raved on. "What in hell is wrong with you, Bradford?"

"Imagine it," Bradford shouted, losing all control. "Imagine it, because that's what you made me do. Do you know what it's like to sit outside a room and hear your wife scream for the services of another man? Do you know what it's like to hear him grunt and pant as he buries himself within her?"

"Why, you hypocritical pervert," Fargo accused, remembering abruptly that he had only stopped by to make sure Bradford hadn't decided to lick his wounds at Fort Laramie. "No matter how hard we tried, Belle and I couldn't scandalize an old maid schoolteacher after she'd been exposed to your blathering bullshit. Because compared to you, Bradford, I'm downright wholesome. And as for Belle, you can say what you want about her nature, but I figure you're the one who's unnatural. And that's a fact."

"Of course I'm unnatural," Bradford conceded indignantly. "We live in an unnatural society. In a primitive society a man can worship nature, because he can freely satisfy his sexual urges. The Indian can take one wife or two or three or four. And they have ready access to captive women," Bradford said so matter-of-factly it chilled Fargo's blood.

When Bradford condoned captives he was approving burning, killing, looting, and mutilation. "I don't believe you," Fargo raged. "You kick Belle out, then act incensed about where she goes. But you've got no qualms about condoning rape and murder."

"Those things are part of the natural condition of man, and I plan to live my life as a natural man. Perhaps I should even thank you for relieving me of Annabelle's company—since she did have a tendency to interfere with my plans. But I'm not going to. Annabelle is still my wife," Bradford snarled. "And you had no right to take her to your room. She had no right to go."

"Come off it, Bradford. You didn't even have the decency to marry Belle properly. She's got no legal rights. And her neighbors would delight in turning up their noses at her. She isn't your wife. She's just a whore you bedded in an Arapaho camp."

"I believe in the sanctity of the Arapaho traditions," Bradford claimed.

"Sure," Fargo agreed. "And the Arapaho believe in divorce and polygamy. That might be fine for a squaw, since she's got friends, family, and a tribe to fall back on if it doesn't work out. But where does that leave Belle?"

"Annabelle will find her future catering to the appetites of men as she always has," Bradford pronounced sourly. "She is a woman driven by erotic insatiability and dominated by a concupiscent essence. I married her, but I could not change her."

"Don't give me that shit about Belle being your wife," Fargo jeered. "You tossed her out as easily as the dishwater."

"Annabelle is an adulterous woman," Bradford declared self-righteously. "And there are no cultural societies known to anthropologists in which licentious women are deemed acceptable mates."

"Oh, Jesus," Fargo cursed. "How do you come up

with this gibberish? And why am I arguing with you? I'd do as well trying to lure the Pope away from the church.''

"Yes," Bradford affirmed. "I agree that you have little talent for debate, and therefore you could never sway either the Pope or myself. But how much more unfortunate it is for you that your true talent lies in luring women from their spouses. Because I'm afraid, Skye Fargo, that you'll find returning my straying wife more difficult than you found taking her.''

"Is that what you think I'm trying to do?" Fargo demanded.

"Isn't it? Aren't you really here because you've found yourself in the inconvenient position of finding that your unavailable married lover has suddenly become available?''

"Hell, no. I only came out here to see what you were planning to do about the treason charge.''

"A most unlikely story, Fargo, since you show an obviously voyeuristic interest in my relationship with Annabelle.''

"Me?" Fargo spluttered. "I'm not the one who jacks off in hotel corridors.''

Bradford turned a pasty gray and reeled away from the doorway while Fargo gaped after him, realizing he had come far too close to the truth.

Over Fargo's shoulder, greening grasses ruffled in the warm breeze and sunshine sparkled off the petals of yellow and blue prairie blossoms. His Ovaro seemed content to graze, but the day was fair and the road was beckoning. Minnesota was out there, waiting.

But Fargo couldn't make himself mount up and ride off. He just couldn't dismiss Bradford that simply. Maybe it was because he still had that vague feeling that there was something that Belle wasn't telling him.

"Goddamn you, Belle, when I see you again, you're going to explain to me how in hell you ever found this one," Fargo muttered as he got up and went inside.

Belle had told the truth about her temper. One of the chairs was tipped over and broken plates littered the floor. Bradford sat in the other chair with an elbow on the table and his forehead in his hand. With his other hand he tilted a whiskey bottle to his lips. Throwing back his head, Bradford quaffed the cheap stuff down.

"That might not be a bad idea," Fargo commented dryly. "A little hair of the dog that bit you. But if you keep going at it like that you're going to feel worse, not better."

Bradford glanced over at Fargo, and his gaze focused slowly behind a veil of tears. Fargo might have felt sorry for Bradford if the man wasn't such an ass. But what kind of man would sit outside a bedroom door and masturbate while his woman was inside?

Bradford looked around dazedly, finally fixing his gaze on an overturned coffee canister. Dry black grounds trailed across the counter and powdered the floor. "This is all your fault," he told Fargo.

"My fault?" Fargo snorted. "And just how is it you get away with acting like a brainless rooster while blaming everybody else?"

"Because I didn't commit adultery. Annabelle did. With you," he added hotly.

Fargo glared at Bradford, feeling that it should be totally unnecessary to remind the poet that a real marriage was a prerequisite to a charge of adultery.

"And I loved her," Bradford shouted.

"Is that why you tried to break her jaw?"

"She deceived me."

"Belle didn't do anything of the kind," Fargo denied. "She came to my room yesterday morning to try to save your worthless hide. If she came to me for comforting after you threw her out, you've only yourself to blame."

"That's not true."

"It is true," Fargo insisted.

Bradford stood up abruptly and his chair flew backwards. "You lie," he accused. "Do you think I don't know how women feel about men like you? It is no secret that women prefer brawn to brains. What do women care about education and erudition?"

"Erudition?" Fargo laughed. "You think you've got air-yoo-di-tion?" he drawled.

Instead of answering, Bradford threw himself at Fargo and his hands seized Fargo's throat. The strength of the skinny poet was surprising. Fargo gasped for air as he brought his arm up between them.

He thrust his elbow hard into the poet's chest. Bradford coughed but held his iron grip on Fargo's neck. Fingers bit into Fargo's gullet, threatening to crush his windpipe. He was getting dizzy from lack of air and the pain choked him. Fargo jerked his knee up, slamming it into Bradford's groin.

Doubled over and clutching his balls with both hands, the poet reeled away. And Fargo couldn't help but laugh. "What's the matter, Bradford?" he taunted. "Think I might have ruined your plans? I figure you'll be all right this time. But if you're not real careful in the future—you just might have to disappoint all those wives and captive women. It'd be a damn shame."

Bradford heaved for air before he finally straightened. Whirling back toward Fargo, he staggered sideways. The effects of a hangover plus the six or eight ounces of whiskey he'd chugged only moments earlier were apparent. Trying to clear his head, Bradford shook like a wet dog. Suddenly leaning forward, he charged.

Bradford's skull rammed into Fargo's stomach, momentarily leaving the Trailsman breathless. Bradford pulled back his arm to deliver a right hook, but his motion was slow. Fargo jumped to the side and Bradford stumbled, careening into the wall.

Turning around, the poet leaned his back against the rough-hewn surface. He was panting like an overtaxed racehorse, but the rage still glinted in his eyes.

"What's the matter, Bradford?" Fargo mocked. "Am I harder to catch than Belle?"

Bradford swooped down and grabbed up the overturned chair at his side. Swinging it around, he hurled it at Fargo, but Fargo sidestepped the projectile easily. Cautiously, with his eyes on the Trailsman, the poet edged toward the cupboard. Fargo made no attempt to stop him.

Bradford seized a frying pan. It flew across the room, crashing harmlessly into the wall a good two feet to Fargo's right. A crock, a cooking pot, a tea canister, and a bowl followed in quick succession, all of them missing their mark.

Due to Belle's temper, there weren't any plates available, and the poet was down to measuring cups and spatulas when he seized upon the knives. With a wild cry of triumph Bradford held up a huge wooden-handled butcher knife.

Getting ready to dive, Fargo eyed Bradford warily. But the poet hadn't the least notion on how to throw a knife. The blade dropped out of the air and thudded uselessly on the table between them.

"You'd better watch out," Fargo laughed as another knife flew at him, handle first. "I've got a notion I can solve this whole debate on whether Belle's really married to you or not by making her a widow."

Bradford leaned heavily on the cupboard behind him while he huffed and puffed. There wasn't a loose object left on his side of the room, but his eyes still gleamed insanely as he scowled at Fargo.

"If this is how you normally behave," Fargo ragged him, "you're going to need four wives just to clean up after you."

With a scream of rage Bradford dived into the table. His right arm came up under it, thrusting it over. Momentarily distracted, Fargo watched the table as it landed on its end.

"Shit," he swore, turning back just as Bradford's head rammed into his gut.

Losing his balance, Fargo fell backward, and the window behind him exploded into a thousand pieces. With dizzying speed he landed in the yard and a sharp shard of glass pierced his shoulder. Bradford landed on top of Fargo, and his weight, slight as it was, knocked the wind out of the Trailsman.

Taking advantage of a cushioned landing, the poet sat up immediately and straddled Fargo. His hands clamped down on the Trailsman's neck, and his eyes bulged with hatred. Bradford's lips drew back as he tightened his hold, baring his teeth like a ravaging, scrawny wolf. His grip crushed down.

"Why, you son of a bitch," Fargo rasped, seeing red as he clenched his fist.

Fargo slammed his fist into Bradford's jaw, but Bradford held on relentlessly. Fargo belted Bradford again, swinging into Bradford's narrow, aristocratic beak. Blood sprayed from the gaunt poet's nostrils, but the blow was too weak to displace Bradford. Gasping for air, Fargo twisted desperately to the side as he delivered another blow. Surprised by the movement beneath him, the drunken poet toppled.

Not daring to hesitate, Fargo gasped in oxygen as he rolled out of Bradford's reach. Bits of broken glass knifed through his shirt, and his chest wheezed like a laboring bellows. Still dizzy and winded, the Trailsman scrambled to his feet several yards away from the downed poet.

Bent over and panting, Fargo watched in amazement as Bradford clambered into a crawling position, seemingly oblivious to the glass cutting his palms. The poet didn't know a thing about fighting, but he was as persistent as a maddened bull.

The cheap whiskey was wreaking its havoc, however. Bradford struggled to his feet and staggered toward Fargo. Bradford swung but Fargo feinted, and the poet hurtled past, sprawling face forward onto the prairie sod. He lay there for several minutes before attempting to shamble up.

Bradford pushed himself up on his knees, swaying as his thin chest pumped for air. Blood streamed from his nose, and blood stained his pants as he wiped off his sweaty palms. There wasn't any spark left in the poet's brown eyes, but he scrambled up just the same.

Bradford lumbered forward and swung hard, but his fist barely grazed Fargo's shoulder. Tired of the game, the Trailsman delivered a stunning left hook. Bradford flew backwards, and his full length bounced on the springy turf.

Flat on his back, Bradford swiped at his face with his hand, trying to clear the sweat from his eyes, but he only succeeded in smearing blood across his brow. The poet tried to sit up, but fell back immediately, groaning.

Fargo dropped down a few yards away to let the breeze dry his perspiration-soaked body while the fresh air cleared his head. White clouds billowed over rolling grassland that was empty for as far as the eye could see. Scanning the horizon to the northeast, Fargo felt he should be able to see all the way to the timberlands of Minnesota. But there was nothing out there.

A sudden movement out of the corner of his eye caught Fargo's attention. "Goddamn it," he cursed as he jumped to his feet. "Why can't that man know when to give up?"

Barely able to stay upright, Bradford careened toward the scrap pile next to the cabin. Fargo hurried to cut him off, but it was too late.

"I've got you now," Bradford screamed as he clutched a wicked-looking board in his bleeding hands. Long, rusty nails protruded from the wood.

"Aw, shit," Fargo spat as Bradford swung the board back.

The poet flailed wildly, slinging the board from side to side as he advanced on the Trailsman. And Fargo backed up, looking for an opening while staying just out of reach. The poet thrashed furiously and blindly, staggering with each swing.

"You look like a berserk windmill," Fargo jeered, hopping aside as Bradford lashed out angrily.

"What's wrong with you anyway?" Fargo needled contemptuously. "You flounder and jerk around like a landed trout."

Just as Fargo expected him to, Bradford reacted violently, twirling as the board he wielded swung him around. Fargo moved in quickly and shoved him. The poet stumbled, dropping the board to retain his balance, and Fargo swooped in to slam a fist into Bradford's belly.

Bradford teetered and Fargo landed another punch on his jaw. There was nothing left in Bradford's gaze but confusion, yet incredibly enough, Bradford stayed up. He was like a tree struck by lightning, too stupid to know that it was all over and there wasn't any point in standing around.

Weakly Bradford grabbed for Fargo, unerringly going for his throat. But the poet was unsteady. He fell forward and his arms shot out over Fargo's shoulders. For a moment Bradford felt more like a sleeping dancing partner than an unstoppable adversary. Fargo shook him off and Bradford fell face forward in the grass.

Grasping Bradford by the hair, Fargo pulled the poet's head back. "Listen to me, Bradford," the Trailsman commanded menacingly, shaking the poet's head until a groan resounded. "You're not going to Fort Laramie until after I come back from Minnesota. And you're not going to touch Belle. If I hear you've hurt Belle, you'll wish they'd hanged you. I'll get you even if you try to hide in jail at Fort Laramie. And I'll be damned if you won't wish it was the Apache who had your scrawny hide. You hear me?" Fargo demanded.

Moaning, Bradford rolled onto his side. Then suddenly he was sobbing like a baby. "I loved her," he gasped. Reaching out, Bradford grabbed Fargo's shirt front. "Oh, God, I loved her," he choked. Bradford had gone back to having that puppy-dog look in his eyes, and his grip on Fargo's shirt was beseeching rather than hostile. "Why?" he whispered. "Why did you have to take her away from me?"

Except for that strange kind of hangdog appeal Fargo had noted the first time he had encountered Bradford, the poet wasn't a pretty sight. His nose was still trickling blood, and blood was matted in his hair. His hands were even messier. Fargo's shirt was lapping up the blood from the poet's right palm.

And the left side of Bradford's face was swelling up fast. Fargo's chest felt sticky and warm with Bradford's blood. And there was so much grass stuck in Bradford's shirt from sliding face first on the ground that he could have been a scarecrow. Belle wouldn't have liked it, Fargo thought with a twinge. Irritably he helped the poet up and dragged him inside.

"Goddamn it," Fargo muttered as he lurched into the bedroom with Bradford weighing on his arm. "That woman is making me soft."

Fargo pushed Bradford unceremoniously onto the bed before he went back out to the kitchen to find soap and water and something that would make do for bandaging.

6

Skye Fargo stood in a doorway at Fort Ridgely, Minnesota, facing an army clerk. "I'd like to see Captain Bannister," he announced.

"Certainly," the clerk answered crisply. "Could you state the nature of your business so that I can announce you, sir?"

"Sure. I'm Skye Fargo, and I've come from Fort Laramie to look into the whereabouts of a Mrs. Elizabeth Frasier."

A flash of something akin to mirth lit the clerk's eyes and a smile played on his lips as he exchanged a look with the young man at the closest desk. The room was crowded with battered desks.

To Fargo's confusion the five young men working there all turned to look up at him; they seemed to be trying not to laugh. Fargo's clerk was suddenly all business again. "Of course, sir," he said. "Captain Bannister is definitely the man you need to see. He's expecting you."

Fargo followed the clerk to the door of a tiny office. "Mr. Fargo has arrived, sir," the clerk announced as Fargo stepped past him.

"I'm Skye Fargo," he told Captain Bannister, watching for the officer's amused reaction. Fargo wondered uncomfortably whether there was a smudge of black or something equally embarrassing on his face. But Captain Bannister didn't smile when Fargo explained his mission. "I was sent from Fort Laramie to inquire into the whereabouts of a Mrs. Elizabeth Frasier."

"Yes," the officer agreed as he stood up to greet Fargo. "But I'm afraid your plans have been changed. Mrs. Frasier has been found."

72

"Is she alive?" Fargo demanded.

"Oh, yes, most definitely," the captain informed Fargo sourly.

"You don't seem too happy about it," Fargo observed.

"No, I'm not," he admitted. "But of course, I'm not nearly as unhappy about it as you're going to be." The captain administered a brief, dry-palmed shake to Fargo's hand. "Would you care to sit down, Mr. Fargo?" he asked as the clerk slid a chair in place behind Fargo, then vanished.

More puzzled than before, Fargo sat down, eyeing the dour-faced captain speculatively. Bannister was fair-haired and handsome. He was also square-jawed and impeccably groomed, but his pale blue eyes radiated all the warmth of a rattler.

"Mrs. Frasier is unwell?" Fargo hazarded, wondering how the general was going to react if his daughter had been found with permanent scars or even worse, some kind of mental derangement. Those problems were pretty standard among former Indian captives.

"Oh, no," Bannister replied. "Actually, she appears to be uncommonly healthy. Or, since I am not a medical man competent to make such judgments, perhaps I should just say that she's well enough to be unforgettably shrill. But then you'll find that out soon enough. Fort Laramie has wired, requesting that you escort her on her way west."

"Me?" Fargo said.

"Yes," the officer asserted, tossing several papers Fargo's way. Fargo picked them up and glanced at them. They were messages to him from Whitcombe.

"But the truth is," Bannister ground out bitterly, "that I don't know what you're doing here, and I certainly don't know why this is a military matter. I've been plagued with reports on Mrs. Frasier and I've already wasted a good deal of precious time searching for her. I am not the woman's keeper. I find this all highly irregular," he complained. "And I don't mind telling you, Mr. Fargo, that I am thoroughly sick of Mrs. Elizabeth Frasier, and I'll be gratified if you'll just get her out of here at the earliest opportunity."

"But I didn't sign on to escort a missionary lady across the country," Fargo objected.

"That's your problem, not mine," Bannister pronounced gleefully.

"Is she really that bad?" Fargo asked, not quite believing the obvious anger Bannister displayed.

"Is she really that bad?" Bannister laughed derisively. "When it comes to Mrs. Frasier, I'm afraid the truth defies description. But I can tell you that she's the most nagging, screeching, obnoxious harridan that I've ever had the misfortune of encountering. The woman's a shrew, a termagant, a complete and utter virago. She's worse than her father. You have met her father, haven't you?" Bannister demanded.

Fargo nodded.

"Well, she's as arrogant, obtrusive, and interfering as he is. And she's damn near as big, a veritable amazon, larger than life and more raucous than a flock of squawking magpies. Do you know what she did?" Bannister demanded.

Fargo wasn't getting a picture of someone he wanted to accompany back to Fort Laramie, but he couldn't quite forget the bag of silver awaiting him there. He sighed. "No, I don't know what she did," he told Bannister quietly, as he wondered why he hadn't been hired to do something simple, like fighting Indians.

"That woman came in here demanding to see our files. When I denied her access to them, she marched right down to the clerk's office and tipped the cabinets over, tossing paper everywhere. When I restrained her and brought her back here, she attacked me physically. And then she set fire to my desk."

Even though he wasn't anxious to meet the woman, Fargo had trouble suppressing a smile. For the first time he understood the laughter in the clerk's office. It was impossible to imagine the cold-eyed, clean-cut, well-groomed Captain Bannister being attacked by a raging harpy and not see the humor in it.

"Just out of curiosity, where was it that Mrs. Frasier's been hiding? Where'd you find her? You didn't mention that."

"We didn't find her. She came here. And as for where she was—do you think the woman would tell us that? She's absolutely uncontrollable, uncooperative, and insubordinate. Wherever she was, I only wish she had chosen to stay there."

"And where is she now?" Fargo asked reluctantly, not entirely sure he wanted to know.

"On the reservation," Bannister answered. "I have duly informed her that her presence there was most improper. The government has not provided those lands to house quarrelsome, sharp-tongued females, but Mrs. Frasier is difficult to deter."

Thanking the officer for his time, Fargo took his leave, but stopped at the clerks' office on his way out. All five soldiers stared at Fargo expectantly.

"I wondered what you could tell me about Elizabeth Frasier," Fargo announced.

The young men glanced at each other nervously. Finally one redheaded youth got up and closed the door. Then, unable to restrain themselves further, they all burst into laughter.

"She sure is something," the redhead guffawed.

"Well, she sure got to Bannister," another clerk laughed. "That's for certain."

"You should have seed it," one of the men told Fargo. "She latched right onto Bannister, clinging to his hair and trying to bite off one of his ears. She hung right on him, too, with her skirts tossed up and her legs wrapped around the captain's waist. She was clawing up a storm, and it was all Bannister could do to cover his face," the young, towheaded speaker recounted exuberantly. "I'll reckon the captain's got more than a few marks on his arms and chest, though," he finished as his ribald laughter choked off words.

"Then when Jones and Mercer managed to pull her off," the redhead elucidated, "she stood there as primly as you please, towering over Bannister while she straightened her skirt. She acted as regal and as haughty as a queen, the way she stared down on him."

"At least until she threw that lit match onto Bannister's desk," the towhead added. "Happened so fast, none of

75

us seed it coming. I reckon we was distracted. Leastwise, none of us ever seed that lucifer till the captain's papers were flaming.''

"She's that bad?" Fargo mumbled miserably.

"Oh, she's awesome, sir," the redhead enthused.

"And she's taller than any woman who ever walked," another soldier laughed.

"More than a match for our captain, that's for certain," the redhead chimed in.

"Why, I reckon if Jones and Mercer hadn't stepped in," the towhead concluded, "she would have taken him."

They were all laughing too much to offer any more information, so Fargo left. He had already taken several weeks to ride to Minnesota, stopping here and there to make inquiries about the Sioux. But now that he knew Elizabeth Frasier was in no danger, Fargo wasn't in any hurry.

He headed east toward Mankato, thinking he could do well with a few days' stopover at a hotel. A couple of hot baths and a willing woman might brighten his outlook. Fargo could use a boost because the prospect of escorting a shrill, giant missionary lady to Ft. Laramie didn't enchant him.

The landscape was prairie dotted with forest. Fargo went out of his way to ride through wooded areas where dappled sunshine filtered down through tender green foliage. It was easy to see why the Santee Sioux were reputed to be so quiet and uncomplaining. Their surroundings were a lot different than the parched, broiling canyonlands of the Apache.

On a warm day in May, Minnesota seemed a shady and peaceful place. Already the prairie grasses were taller than Fargo had seen them grow anywhere else, and it was still early in the season. Minnesota probably wasn't too friendly in the winter, but then it couldn't get any more hostile than a Nebraska blizzard. For a while he rode beside the wide, placid Minnesota River, a trail of sorts, where emigrants arrived by steamboat rather than wagon. Not feeling sociable, Fargo left the river before he got to where the little German settlement of New Ulm sat on the opposite bank.

As he rode past another lake, Fargo slowed the Ovaro. It was a big one this time. A ridge of timber rose on the opposite bank, but the trees were so far away they dissolved into a haze of gray-green beyond the vivid expanse of blue. Fargo had been riding past lakes for days, and it didn't seem fair.

There had to be more lakes in Minnesota than anyone needed or could even figure out what to do with. And just one of their itsy-bitsy ones would have been real handy down south of the Cimarron. If only nature had spared a couple of those lakes for the lands of the Navaho, the Kiowa, the Comanche, and the Apache, maybe things would have been easier down there. One thing was certain, Minnesota never would have missed them.

But on the other hand, lakes brought more white folks than desert did, more white folks than the southwestern Indians would tolerate. They brought more white folks than even Fargo liked. In Minnesota there were farms hidden most everywhere, nice places on beautiful land with clear lakes and good soil.

But over the years Fargo supposed he had come to appreciate something harsher, more formidable: scree and shale, steep slopes and slick rock, high peaks and barren mesas, cactus and bristlecone, hawks, buzzards, coyotes, jackrabbits, even rattlers. He liked lonesome land. It suited his ways.

Minnesota wasn't like that, but it was a nice place to visit. And Mankato proved to be real hospitable. In short order Fargo found his bath and a little, brown-haired widow who claimed to be a seamstress but didn't take in any sewing. She had nothing against letting him in the back door, however, if it was after midnight and the neighbors wouldn't notice.

As it turned out, Fargo overstayed his intentions. After a week in Mankato he was sitting in a saloon, telling himself that he couldn't just stay there forever, even if it had turned out to be a pleasant place.

It was still early in the evening and there weren't too many customers. Fargo watched the bartender polish the glasses. It wasn't a fancy place. The glass the bartender was vigorously buffing with a tea towel was really a cracked preserves jar, so Fargo figured the man was only biding his time until there was something better to do.

"You happen to know Captain Bannister?" Fargo finally asked.

The bartender set the jar down and leaned on the bar, pleased to have found another distraction. Middle-aged, bald, and plump, the man was big enough to act as a bouncer if necessary. Shaggy red eyebrows over squinty eyes and a bushy handlebar mustache over a mouth that naturally turned down at the corners made him look tougher than he probably was.

"I've seen Captain Bannister," he said. "I don't know him."

"You wouldn't happen to know a woman named Elizabeth Frasier, would you?"

"Now, everybody's heard of her." The bartender grinned. "She's the missionary lady. The one who's always telling the uppity folks around here where to get off. I don't know her, but I'd sure like to meet her. She's lit into some of my most unfavorite people."

"You mean, you think you'd like her?" Fargo asked.

With a smile on his face the burly bartender looked about as fierce as a teddy bear. "I suspect not," he laughed. "From what I hear, nobody can get along with her. But at least she ain't afraid to pick on them that's most deserving. So I guess I'd like to meet her, regardless. Even if it's just to see if she's as big as they say she is."

Laughing, the bartender moved away to serve another customer, and Fargo took his drink and his bottle to a small round table. He felt trapped. He hadn't agreed to escort a missionary anywhere, especially an ornery missionary. But he suspected Whitcombe wouldn't give him another dollar if he didn't. Which wasn't fair since Fargo had ridden all the way out to Santee country to find her.

"And I did find her," he declared. It wasn't his fault if Fort Ridgely had found her first.

And yet this whole job Whitcombe had handed him was becoming ridiculous. In all probability, now that his daughter was found, General Colson would calm down enough to continue his tour of inspection and forget about harassing Fort Laramie and the Sioux. And once he was back to work, it was doubtful the general would find the time to plague a transcendentalist poet he'd taken a dislike to.

In which case, Fargo had wasted a trip out to see Bradford. And all the irritation he had put up with from Bradford had been totally unnecessary. For a moment a stray memory of Belle brought a smile, but it disappeared as quickly as it came.

He still wasn't sure Belle was safe with Bradford; he had a bad feeling about it, a feeling he couldn't shake. Which made things worse, since Fargo knew he was going to have to go back to check on Belle even if he didn't have to return to save Bradford's ass. Sure, Whitcombe had paid him, but a man felt kind of silly when his work turned out to be so frivolous. And now they wanted him to nursemaid a lady missionary.

There hadn't been any point in reading all Bradford's lousy poetry. There hadn't been any point in rambling all over Nebraska, and there hadn't been any point in meeting Bradford, talking to Bradford, listening to Bradford, or fighting with Bradford.

Fargo couldn't help being glad he'd seen Belle, but on the other hand, that sure hadn't worked out well. So he supposed there hadn't been any point in seeing Belle, either, at least right then, since he could have waited to see her until she was free. With the sort of men she picked, her eventual freedom always seemed inevitable.

Unfortunately, there was a point in taking Elizabeth Frasier back to Ft. Laramie. It meant Whitcombe would hand over the bag of silver. The money wouldn't make up for the bothersome nature of Fargo's long trip, but Fargo was now in Minnesota. After he'd come so far, it seemed foolish to turn around without any possibility of getting paid.

The unsteady table tilted awkwardly as Fargo rested his elbows. Scowling, he leaned back in his chair.

"Excuse me, sir," a man said hesitantly.

A dapper little man sporting a gray suit, a derby hat,

a brocaded vest, and a silver watch fob stood over Fargo, but just barely. Standing while Fargo sat, the nervous man had about four inches on the Trailsman.

"Yes," he acknowledged, standing up to extend his hand in a gesture of friendship. "I'm Fargo. Skye Fargo."

The man shaking Fargo's hand wasn't much more than a midget. His hand was child-sized and soft, and the top of his head just about reached the level of the middle button on Fargo's shirt. "I'm Barton Hughes, a reporter with the *Boston Transcript*," he said. "I've been traveling out here to do a story on my impressions of the West. But my editor asked me to contact Elizabeth Frasier while I was in this area. I couldn't help but overhear your conversation with the bartender, and I have met Mrs. Frasier," Hughes finished uncertainly.

"What did you think of her?" Fargo broke in.

"I'm afraid I found her to be most intimidating. I really didn't know what to make of her. I thought perhaps you could help me."

"I doubt it," Fargo admitted. He sat down.

Hughes took the seat across from him, looking down dubiously before easing daintily onto the chair, as if he were afraid it wasn't quite clean. "But then I don't really understand why you were sent to talk to Mrs. Frasier. She's from Boston, though, isn't she?" Fargo mused. "Your editor a friend of hers?"

"Oh, no, sir. My editor has never met her. That's why he sent me."

"Sure," Fargo said as he tried to puzzle out whether that made any sense. He picked up the whiskey bottle and waved it at Hughes's empty glass. "Want some?"

Hughes's eyes grew round, and he flinched back as he covered his glass with his hand. "Oh, no, sir. I'm a temperance man, myself. But I wouldn't refuse to drink with you," he added hurriedly. "I've heard that it's an insult to refuse to drink with a man in the West." The little man smiled apprehensively. "I don't touch distilled spirits, but I find wine quite satisfying. Bartender," Hughes called, his voice raising an octave.

"Hell, I didn't know they had wine in places like this."

Fargo shrugged. If the saloon didn't have wine the bartender would serve Hughes watered-down beer and tell him it was champagne.

Hughes didn't complain. The bartender set down his drink, winking at Fargo, and Hughes smiled broadly as he sniffed it. While he watched the little man wipe off the rim of his "champagne" glass with his handkerchief, Fargo couldn't help but wonder what that editor in Boston had been thinking.

Hughes seemed an unlikely sort to send out West. He didn't look like he could hold up to so much as hearing about Indians and rattlesnakes, let alone facing them. But then again, maybe he was checking out the restaurants or some such thing.

To Hughes that would seem dangerous enough. He sipped the beer as if he feared it contained cyanide, but he drank it, regardless. Probably that was only because he believed Fargo would be even more dangerous than tainted alcohol if he didn't drink it.

Intimidating Barton Hughes didn't take much, but Fargo wondered why anyone would bother. "Did Mrs. Frasier do something to offend you?" he asked.

"Oh, no," Hughes denied. "But she and her friends seemed to be . . ." Hughes paused, narrowing his eyes thoughtfully as if he wasn't quite sure what Elizabeth Frasier seemed to be. "Feuding with the traders," he finished. "At least they were quite belligerent."

"Belligerent?"

"Oh, yes. Mrs. Frasier even shot one of the trader's horses. Well, perhaps she didn't. I'm afraid I'm not at all familiar with firearms. But she did point her rifle at the poor beast, and he let out a terrible bellow and stampeded away with the wagon and that poor trader and his wife. Why it's a wonder that wagon didn't overturn. Although afterward the horse didn't appear to be injured in any way."

"Birdshot," Fargo concluded. "From a distance. But you still haven't told me why you wanted to talk to her."

"Why, because she's been sending our paper the most startling letters, claiming that the traders take Indian allotments without supplying goods. Claiming that Indians are starving. Claiming that Indian children are being stolen and pressed into servitude. Claiming that the women on the reservation are frequently abused by men passing through. My editor thought I should look into those charges.''

"You?'' Fargo blurted.

"Why, yes. But of course, Mrs. Frasier is a very adequate writer. If we find her character trustworthy she can supply the stories.''

"Oh, I'm sure the stories are true,'' Fargo said. "That's the way of it out here. The Indians terrorize the whites, or the whites terrorize the Indians. The Santees have been pretty peaceful, so no doubt a lot of the folks dealing with them have gotten out of line. That's the way it works.''

"You can't mean that, Mr. Fargo.''

"Mr. Hughes, anyone out West will tell you that. Why don't you ask some other reporters? A lot of the papers out here have tried to point out that some of the Indian agencies are stealing the Indians blind. There's a lot of profit to be made in it.''

"But that's uncivilized,'' Hughes protested.

"Mr. Hughes, folks don't come out West because they want to be civilized. They come out here because they want to be rich.''

"I'm still not sure,'' Hughes objected, wringing his hands as he spoke. "It was quite obvious that Mrs. Frasier personally disliked the traders. And westerners are prone to exaggerate.''

"Are you calling westerners liars, Mr. Hughes?'' Fargo asked coldly.

"Oh, no. Oh, no,'' the little man choked.

"All right,'' Fargo excused him. "Although actually some are,'' he confessed, smiling. "But I'm not, and you can believe what I tell you. The truth is, I don't know a lot about the Santees. But I do know there's a bounty on Apache scalps. Take 'em in and they pay you for 'em. And I know there used to be a lot of Indians in California. But now there are hardly any, and it isn't any secret that some of those who weren't shot were sold. Or that one hell of a lot of their women ended up in brothels.''

"Mr. Fargo, surely you are talking about exceptions."

"Sure, a few thousand exceptions. Look, it probably isn't that bad here. But there's no question that too many thieves see the Indians as easy prey, and too many Indian agents are thieves. So if you were an Indian, it might feel that bad. And if you were a missionary lady, you'd probably try to do something about it. If you think your newspaper might change things, then print Mrs. Frasier's stories."

"But what if they're not accurate?" Hughes asked timidly. "I talked to several agents and traders. They seemed like reasonable people. To blame the problems of the Indians on traders might not be fair. It was obvious, even on the short visit I made, that the Indians are not totally content with reservation life, but perhaps that's to be expected since they were nomadic savages until only recently. I'm afraid that Mrs. Frasier and the other missionaries are really too close to the Indians to be objective."

"Goddamn it, I'm no bleeding heart," Fargo chafed. "I've fought Indians, I've killed Indians, I've even scalped them a time or two." Fargo saw Hughes blanch and he hastened to explain. "Hey, when you get attacked in Indian country, you kill, and if there's any chance the poor devil's brothers don't know who you are, you don't leave a full head of hair to advertise that you're a white man. Though, God knows, a lot of white men enjoy taking scalps."

Fargo glared at Hughes. "I'm no missionary," he told him icily. "But it isn't fair to pick on peaceful Indians. I understand how it happens—too many people harbor too many fears and too much hate. The people out here who haven't had trouble with Indians have heard too many stories about them. Most folks know what's going on; they know of crooked agents and thieving traders. But they don't do anything. I understand that, but it doesn't make it right."

"I don't know," Hughes mumbled. "But you can be certain I'll take what you've said into consideration."

"You don't know," Fargo thundered. "I just told you."

Hughes jumped out of his chair. "Yes," he agreed as he backed away. "And I want to thank you for your time." About halfway to the door Hughes turned around and scurried out as if Fargo was a temperamental grizzly and was likely to chase him.

The thought did cross Fargo's mind. His mood had been bad enough before the little man had come along. "I hope that man runs into a nest of rattlers," he brooded aloud. "Or a party of Comanche. Or eats green chile in Santa Fe. That would probably be enough to do him in."

"Who do you want to do in, darlin'?" a husky voice asked.

"Nobody," Fargo confessed. "I was just talking to myself."

"About Barton Hughes, I'd guess. He tends to get on everyone's nerves."

"You know him?"

"He's been around for a few weeks. He hates it here. Sits on the chairs as if we polished them with lard. But he claims he needs to soak up the atmosphere. That's about all the man soaks up. In two weeks he hasn't ordered more than three drinks."

Fargo stared up at the auburn-haired woman. She must have really been something once, and at thirty-seven or so she was still a lot more than most. Her age showed in the way her makeup made her skin look fragile rather than smooth, but her face was still pretty and her curves were just about perfect beneath her tight, low-cut black velvet gown.

"Were you enjoying talking to yourself, or would you rather talk to me?" the woman asked.

"I wouldn't mind talking to you," Fargo answered as he studied the bulge of bosom swelling out of her dress. "But where should we talk? Your place or mine?"

"Mine," she laughed. "It's closer. Right upstairs as a matter of fact."

Marion Sinclair wasn't much of a talker. She led Fargo right through her parlor and into the bedroom. Her place surprised him. There was a piano in the front room, and pianos were rare in the West. Although, like Missouri, Minnesota wasn't a part of the hinterlands, and by Nebraska and Dakota territory standards was comparatively civilized, a piano was still a sign of affluence Fargo hadn't expected to see in the quarters of a small-town prostitute.

Marion lit the lantern on her dresser but turned it down so that the light shining from beyond the milky glass globe was soft and mellow. Without further ado she reached back and unhooked her dress.

The dress was revealing but simple, not gaudy. She had a big brass bed with a quilted coverlet. A fine flowered rug spread over the waxed hardwood floor. Marion opened a huge mahogany wardrobe. Inside were gowns of silk and satin, but there were also two calicoes and a plain blue cotton wrapper. Her place was cozy, not flamboyant.

But the most noticeable thing about it was it wasn't cheap. The burnished wood of the dresser gleamed with hand carving, the drapes were of heavy wine-colored velvet. The chair sitting next to the bed was a little too delicate for Fargo's taste, but it was pretty, with its ornately curved legs and striped satin covering.

The woman had good taste. Even her makeup was subtle, just a bit of powder with a touch of rouge to highlight her lips and cheeks. Fargo probably wouldn't have noticed it at all if she had been a few years younger. Still, her face wasn't lined. There was merely that soft, fragile quality to her skin and a certain, almost sculptured, hollowness to her cheekbones to betray her age.

There was that, and the fact that Fargo was the Trailsman, and he sometimes studied things more than he needed to. Fargo smiled to himself, admitting that he'd been in a nitpicking mood to even look for imperfections in Marion Sinclair, because she sure as hell was not the kind of woman he would have expected to find working in a rough-and-tumble saloon. She had her back turned to him as she hung the velvet dress in the wardrobe.

"I kind of thought there'd be more girls working up here," Fargo commented.

"Oh," she gasped, whirling around and staring before she burst into laughter. "Mr. Fargo, I'm a businesswoman, but I'm definitely not in that business. Neither is my saloon." Her laughter faded as she studied him.

Her manner was frankly appraising. "Generally, I try to make that clear," she told him. "I guess I just got excited about coming upon the handsomest stranger I've seen in a long time." Marion Sinclair's voice held a hint of the South in it, but her husky drawl was as subtle as her place.

Her actions were anything but subtle, however, as she drew her black lace chemise over her head. Stretching languidly, she uncovered flesh Fargo might have thought too pale if it hadn't molded perfect curves. Her well-rounded breasts lifted and then fell back as she dropped her chemise to the floor.

Wearing only a black garter belt and black silk stockings, Marion stood in front of Fargo. She arched one brow inquiringly and humor shimmered in her green eyes. "Well, darlin'?" she said as her gaze traveled down his length. A little smile formed on her lips and her eyes narrowed speculatively as her inspection settled on the region below his belt buckle. "Don't you think it's your turn?"

For a moment she looked just like the cat who had eaten the canary. There was something blatant in her perusal of him, something that made Fargo feel as if he were onstage. She aroused him, but he wasn't about to dance for her.

"Maybe it is my turn," he admitted, but he didn't bother to undress. Unsmiling, Fargo watched her, waiting to see what she would do.

The woman stepped up to Fargo, but for several moments she merely studied his face. Then her fingers grazed his temple, and her thumbs smoothed the lines radiating from his lake-blue eyes, lines that were caused by sun and weather, not age. Sighing, she moved her hands to the buttons of his shirt.

Quickly and efficiently Marion dispatched the shirt, pushing it off his shoulders before she took to stroking his chest. With pursed lips she caressed his skin, pausing to frown at a scar on his shoulder and worry over a nick on his side. She moved unhurriedly, but her breath came faster as her fingers circled, pausing to knead and explore his collarbone, his ribs, his muscles. The woman stared at his bronzed skin as if she were trying to read something written there.

She was sultry and fluid in her motions. Her body undulated like the tide. She looked, she touched, she rubbed, she caressed, she stared, and her breath started catching. Little mewing sounds accompanied the sensuous rolling and stretching of her shoulders. But as far as Fargo was concerned, she didn't stand close enough.

She kept far enough back to survey him, whimpering over every little nick she found while she soothed hurts he hadn't felt in years. Fargo had never known a woman who took such an interest in details. She was unquestionably taken with him. In truth, her devotion was fervent and almost eerie. She had a strange look to her, like someone inspired by a poem or moved by a sunset. And her breathing was positively ragged, mewing out and gasping in.

Marion's tempo was picking up, and she sounded as if she was having a real good time, oohing out and ahing in, and then groaning as if climactic pleasures were only seconds away. Although Fargo couldn't see that she was accomplishing much with all her rubbing and staring, Marion seemed to think she was getting somewhere. One thing was certain, the woman was definitely showing a lot more fascination with his chest than Fargo thought it was due.

Stepping closer, Marion Sinclair pressed her face into Fargo's shoulder and her hips into his pelvis. She rocked and rolled and gyrated against him, and her mewing escalated to outright moaning. Curiosity grabbed a hold of Fargo. Staring down on the woman's head, he wondered just how far she would go without encouragement.

Gritting his teeth, Fargo kept his arms at his sides. He hadn't once so much as tried to reach out and touch her, and yet the woman kept going. Fargo felt his temperature rising and his perspiration flowing as his need surged. But he was caught up in her strange game, and he found himself as fascinated with her peculiarities as she was with his flesh.

Marion slid around behind him. Embracing him, she pressed her hands into his hard abdominal muscles, exploring them diligently as she glided, shimmied, and wiggled against his back. She lapped at his shoulder blades. Her mouth felt hot, but it left behind shivery, drying places on his skin.

Her breasts pressed into him, her nipples circling, shaking and sliding, feeling almost scratchy. She began to arch against him, and her moans turned to cries that sounded far more passionate than her position called for. Her hands dug into his belly, trying to pull him back as she pumped and thrust against his backside.

Her fascination with his body amused Fargo, but he wasn't made of marble. Left to her own devices, Marion Sinclair had been playing with him for the better part of an hour and hadn't gotten beyond his belly. Listening to her drawn-out cries, Fargo decided he had made a tactical error. This lady didn't need a partner, at least not an active one, maybe not even a living one.

He was about to abandon his waiting game when she eased back around him. To Fargo's relief, she dropped to her knees, unhooking his belt as deftly as she had his shirt buttons. She pushed his clothing down slowly, and her hands wisped along his thighs and calves.

But then she threw her arms around his legs and buried her face between them, just above his knees. Her body danced and wove against his legs. She moaned continuously, and her hot, moist breath fanned across his kneecaps.

With her clinging to him that way, Fargo felt as if he was being worshiped by somebody a lot more pagan than the Indians had ever been. Fargo couldn't believe it. Her hips were swaying and rotating, and her moaning was building into an outlandish noise. He stared down at her, absolutely mesmerized.

It was then he realized she was oozing up. She seemed so overexcited and hungry he was tempted to run before her teeth could get anywhere near a sensitive spot. Fortunately, she leaned back. Marion looked as obsessed as ever but not dangerous. She huffed and puffed and moaned, but she was quieting some.

She cupped his genitals in her hands experimentally, as if to weigh them as she scrutinized his assets. Her fingers slid up to grasp his throbbing shaft, tickling, stroking, caressing, and teasing as she gazed on raptly. Not at all sure that he could take any more attention on her part, Fargo sucked in his breath.

Her tongue flicked out and lapped across his shaft. And then she blew cold air on him intentionally. Fargo jerked back and Marion laughed, a low husky laugh. Her warm hands circled him again, and he realized she would play this game as long as she could.

She was driving him crazy. Her hands manipulated his shaft as if it were a needlepoint project. Without so much as glancing up at his face once, she tugged, she squeezed, and she fingered. She seemed to have forgotten Fargo entirely as she eyed her work avidly, and her noise started rising up again.

Suddenly Marion Sinclair came unglued. She panted and grunted, and pounded her pelvis against his leg while the rest of her shook all over the place. She started tossing her head back and forth. Her breasts jiggled against his thighs and her shoulders banged into him.

But she knew what she was doing with her hands; Fargo felt it building. His jaw clenched, and his shoulders stiffened. Marion threw her head back and filled the room with a sound he had thought only a coyote could make.

And then she abandoned Fargo altogether. Marion threw herself back. Her knees came up and her shoulders arched. With one hand clamped between her thighs and the other clutching her breast, she writhed on the floor at Fargo's feet.

Fargo felt the throbbing in his groin. He had never seen anything like Marion's passion. Her body was shimmering white, heaving and squirming on the carpet. Her head was thrown so far back that he couldn't see her face, but her auburn hair was a damp, tangled mass framing the too-pale flesh. Her breasts were taut with the nipples pointing straight toward the ceiling, but her belly undulated and rolled and twisted.

While she grunted and groaned and whimpered all at the same time, her hips strained and the muscles of her thighs jerked convulsively, visibly. Her outlandish sounds rolled together into a full-throated bellow, and Marion gasped for air as her body seized up. For a moment she was absolutely rigid, and then she screamed. She screamed so loud, Fargo glanced toward the door, wondering if everybody in the saloon would come to her rescue.

But he couldn't keep his eyes off her for long. She was churning and seething and bouncing, but she was winding down. Marion twisted sideways and her movement slowed again. She brought her knees up to her chest, and her hips settled into a slow serpentine roll. Her ass was turned to Fargo. The pallid flesh circled sensuously beneath the lace of her black garter belt.

The woman lay there at his feet, one hand still clasped between her thighs as her bottom rolled and twitched until finally she sighed. Without one upward glance she got back on her knees and took Fargo's ready organ in her hand. But she didn't do anything with it; she merely stared at it as if she were in a trance.

And Fargo marveled at her—while she just kept gazing at his pecker. She touched it, but softly, her fingers fluttering in their caress. There was sweat glistening on her flesh, and he could smell her musk. She leaned over and kissed his swollen flesh, her lips barely brushing the surface before she sat back. And then she started cooing to it.

Fargo gaped down at her. Never in his life could he remember feeling so hot, so aching, so awed, and so frustrated. The tension spread into his belly and thighs. It ached in his chest.

Even worse, he began to have a strange feeling that her eyes were as warm as her hands. She was staring at him and he could feel it.

"Shit," Fargo breathed. "What are you doing, woman? You've been inspecting that thing more than you would a horse at auction. You planning on riding it or purchasing it?"

Surprised out of her contemplative mood, Marion Sinclair glanced up at Fargo with a look of startled innocence on her face. "Oh, I'm sorry," she apologized. Abruptly her solemnity vanished and she giggled. "We used to own a horse farm—in Kentucky."

90

"We?"

"My husband and me. He died a few years back."

"That's too bad," Fargo responded mechanically as he realized he had let her play her game too long. The tension from waiting was still coiled in his chest; it pulled at his gut and throbbed in his groin.

"It was," she admitted wistfully. "But my husband was thirty years older than me, so it was bound to happen."

Fargo gaped at her, temporarily too astonished to do anything. Right before his eyes the woman had been transformed from a wanton in heat into an ordinary gossip.

Marion Sinclair shook her head as if she could shake away unhappy memories. Then she laughed. "You know, Skye Fargo. There isn't anything I admire more than a fine horse, except a good man," she said as her gaze pointedly returned to his erect shaft. "And you, sir, are a glorious beast."

"I trust you do more than admire," Fargo fumed. "To tell the truth, your way of admiring can be a mite unnerving."

"But not too unnerving," she observed, bounding to her feet. Laughing, she fell back on the bed, still clad in the garter belt and black silk stockings.

Marion thrust her knees apart and Fargo's view of the flesh between her slender, black-clad limbs was unimpeded. She was pulsating, moist, and as ready as he was.

"Now," she begged, twisting her hips up to display even more of her glistening center.

"But I haven't so much as kissed you," he commented.

"Later," she rasped. "You can do that later."

7

Fargo fell on Marion and thrust inside her in one smooth motion. She was an easy woman to please, which was a good thing because he was beyond caring. Grasping her hips, he pounded into her repeatedly.

Marion shrieked and her whole body shuddered from top to toes. Her insides pulsated wildly, and she twisted and bucked and tugged at him.

But Fargo didn't let up. He just grabbed her hips, pinned her in place and slammed into her. She screamed again, a shrill, ear-shattering screech. Her body shook convulsively. Her arms and legs clamped onto him, but the rest of her seethed and tossed and churned. She was tugging and pounding at him inside and out. Feeling the throb of her muscles, he bore down hard.

In one enormous rush Fargo exploded, and the world around him lurched, burst, and faded in a single moment. But only a few minutes passed before Fargo found he was ready to test Marion's appreciation again.

He thought about kissing and stroking her, but he gave one experimental lunge and the woman reacted so fervently he kept hammering. Finally sated, Fargo dropped onto Marion Sinclair's heaving chest. He had barely caught his breath when she squirmed beneath him. Assuming that she was trying to slide out from under him because he was too heavy, Fargo started to roll to one side, but her hands clutched his hips.

Marion tugged down hard, determined to keep him inside of her. Her legs came up to circle his waist and she pressed her hips into his. Her pelvis rotated slowly, and her muscles tightened on his spent organ.

Dazed, Fargo raised himself up on his elbows to stare

down at Marion's face. His weight shifted onto her pelvis, and the woman let out a squeal. Her thighs clamped onto his waist like a vise. While Fargo watched, Marion gasped, trembled, and frothed right up. Her nails bit into his ass and her hips leapt forward. Before Fargo could quite comprehend what was happening, the woman was bouncing and steaming like water on a hot griddle.

"It's so good. It's so good," she moaned, pounding into him as her features contorted with effort. Her mound pressed hard and her innards squeezed at him. "Oh, please," she cried. "I want it. I want more. I want . . ."

"I should have figured," Fargo muttered, but before he could do anything to oblige her, Marion's body spasmed.

She lunged up, screamed, and fell back. "You're so good. You're so fine," she panted.

In truth, Fargo couldn't see that he'd done anything to merit praise. He was still up on his elbows, staring down at her. Her eyes were squeezed shut and her face was flushed, but otherwise she looked like an ordinary woman. She was prettier than most, but she didn't really look unusual. Which just went to show that appearances could be mighty deceiving.

Marion was wet. Her hair was damp, and her skin was shiny. Laughing, Fargo pulled the woman into his arms, but she felt as limp as a wet washrag in his embrace.

Marion opened her eyes and gazed at him. "You're so perfect," she whispered dreamily as a dopey smile transformed her face. She reached out to touch his face with an expression so reverent, Fargo convulsed in laughter.

The woman's persistence had paid off, and Fargo found himself eager, hard, and curiously taken with her even though she had gone on without him. Still laughing, he plunged in deep, but she was so slippery, inside and out, that he almost skidded off of her.

Marion snaked and wiggled against Fargo. She flowed under him, her belly oozing across his muscles as her breasts alternately slid and stuck against his chest.

Fargo drove into her again. She twisted and he skated off to one side. He righted himself, laughing raucously as she clamped him fiercely in her embrace. He hammered down at her, driving in too easily and sliding out too readily. He kept laughing as she reared up again and again, grunting purposefully. Fargo paused for a minute, and Marion clutched him. She rocked into him, pounding his ass with her fists and Fargo laughed even harder.

"Please," she groaned. "I need it. I want it. It's so beautiful. Don't take it away."

"Beautiful?" Fargo repeated dubiously.

She nodded emphatically, while her whole body trembled with enthusiasm.

The woman was as slick as a greased pig at a fair. And Fargo was shaking so hard with laughter, he wasn't sure he could have stayed atop a sawhorse. Marion started pitching and heaving under him.

Fargo rose up over her, fighting to curb his rollicking mirth. She tossed her head back and forth in a frenzy and flailed her shoulders wildly. Her breasts were jouncing with so much vigor, the leaping and capering nipples seemed to be partnered in a dance.

"Why don't we wait a bit?" he suggested when he finally got his laughter under control.

"Oh, no," she begged. "Please no. It feels so good. You don't have to do anything," she rasped. "Just let me have it for a little while longer."

"Sure," Fargo agreed reluctantly, although he thought there would be more reason and just as much pleasure in dipping his organ in hot bathwater at that point.

Figuring he would let her play out her game by herself, Fargo dropped down on Marion wearily. Closing his eyes, he tried to relax, but she was wriggling and squirming so much it was probable that a nest of snakes would have made as comfortable a mattress.

Then to his amazement, her slick innards gripped Fargo, surprising him. Marion's muscles quivered, they twitched, they throbbed. Awed, Fargo propped himself up to stare down at her again.

Marion Sinclair looked enraptured, transported, lost on a private journey all her own. Her eyes were closed, her mouth was open and she kept on drawing in air and drawing in air. Her belly was sucked in tight, and her chest was thrust up high. As Fargo watched, her breasts seemed to swell with her effort.

Then, as if she had been dosed with alum, her insides puckered up around him until suddenly her muscles clamped down so hard on his shaft that Fargo gasped for air himself. Recovering, he pulled out of Marion and drove right back in, deciding as he did so that Marion Sinclair was going on one trip he didn't want to miss.

But as soon as Fargo finished one trip, Marion was taking him on another. He was on his way somewhere when he finally fell asleep from exhaustion, and when he woke up, Marion was pulling him off somewhere else.

As Skye Fargo pulled on his Levis, he glanced over his shoulder at Marion Sinclair. She didn't look altogether happy.

"Is something wrong?" he asked.

"You didn't like it, did you?" she whispered.

"Sure I did," he assured her as he sat on the end of the bed to pull on his boots. Fargo looked at her curiously, wondering why she would think otherwise. He had spent half the night liking the woman and all of the morning. Fargo knew for a fact that he had never liked a woman so much in such a short time in his life.

"I liked it fine," he told her, glancing down at the rug as he tugged on his boot. Sunlight shimmered off the intricately woven gold threads entwining the red and blue flowers. Smiling, Fargo enjoyed a vivid recollection of how Marion's naked body had looked outlined by that carpet the previous evening.

It had been the best damn floor show he'd ever seen, certainly better than the Lola Montez snake dance he had seen when he wasn't much more than a boy. And it had definitely been a lot more titillating than seeing Adah Menken ride out on stage wearing flesh-colored tights. In spite of all the fanfare those women got, Fargo had long since found out that a night spent in was usually a lot more interesting than a night out. Marion Sinclair was a little strange, but she had been real interesting.

"I liked it just fine," he repeated.

"Am I different than other women?" she fretted.

"All people are different from each other," Fargo said.

Then, avoiding what might prove to be an embarrassing discussion, he changed the subject. "What's it like owning a saloon? You do own it, don't you?" he asked.

Her mind still on her performance, Marion nodded vaguely. "I've been thinking about it a lot lately. And I can't figure out how a woman can know if she's normal. She isn't in any position to judge."

"The saloon must be pretty profitable," Fargo plunged on determinedly as his lake-blue gaze shifted from the brass bed to the wardrobe and back again.

"What? Oh, you must be referring to my insurance policy," Marion said. "The furniture comes from the farm. I always held onto it in case of hard times. But whenever hard times came I held onto it for worse times."

"You've had a lot of hard times?" Fargo asked as he studied Marion Sinclair curiously. She had pinned up her hair earlier and put on one of the calico dresses. Without makeup her high cheekbones gave her a refined, genteel look. If she hadn't been sitting on a bed with him, Fargo would have guessed her to be a very pretty but overly proper housewife.

"I've had my share of bad times, I guess." Marion smiled wistfully. "I married the man my parents wanted me to. He was respectable, kind, and well-off, but not young. He developed a heart condition and was bedridden within five years. I couldn't take care of the farm and him and the children too. We lost it."

"You have children?"

"Three," she answered. "They live with my parents, but I support them. Poor Joshua would roll over in his grave if he knew I owned a saloon. But it was a good investment. And the truth is," she admitted sheepishly, "when I came up here to visit an old friend, I was ready to take worse work."

"It seems to me, you do all right," Fargo said, noting the little worry lines etched on her forehead.

"At first it was hard, leaving the children behind. But they're older now and they understand a little better. And I spend two months with them every year," she announced proudly. "Besides, the way things were going, we would have used up everything we had. Then I lucked onto the saloon. I was all ready to go to work here, the way you thought I worked here, when I found out the saloon would only cost me half as much as the stores I'd looked into. And the inventory for it cost me a lot less than the inventory for a mercantile.''

"You don't have to explain it to me," Fargo told her gently.

"I know. It's just that . . ." Marion Sinclair shrugged and laughed apologetically. "Oh, hell," she said. "It's just that the last man I had up here upset me so much, I haven't had anyone else up in weeks. He told me I was unnatural. I don't know what I did to Captain Bannister, but he called me all sorts of terrible names and then he ran right out of here without his clothes. Well, he did take his clothes," she admitted. "But he must have put them on in the stairwell."

"Bannister?" Fargo laughed.

"You know him?" Marion gasped, blushing to the roots of her hair. "Oh, dear," she whispered. "How embarrassing. I know he isn't a very pleasant man, but . . ."

Fargo laughed even harder.

"Oh, he is right, isn't he?" she blurted. "I am peculiar. Sometimes when I'm working downstairs, something just comes over me and I get so brazen, I . . ." Marion faltered. "I know women with children aren't supposed to want men so much, but I need . . . Oh, dear," she mumbled again. "I just can't seem to help it. I even knew Captain Bannister wasn't very nice. But he's so pretty," she wailed.

"Pretty?" Fargo guffawed. "Is that what you think I am?"

"Oh, no," she denied, glancing up at Fargo and then back down at her folded hands in her lap.

Glimpsing the tears in her eyes, Fargo sobered instantly.

"You're everything," she whispered. "You're perfect."

"Don't I wish," Fargo countered. "Look, I wasn't laughing at you. It was just the idea of Bannister . . ."

"That's all right," she assured Fargo hastily.

"You know, Bannister isn't the only man I've met recently who doesn't know how to appreciate a good woman," Fargo commented as he thought of Bradford. "I'm afraid you're bound to run into one now and again. Don't you think it'd be best to ignore the ones who don't like you, and enjoy the ones who do?"

Marion nodded glumly. "I never claimed to be a good wife or mother," she persisted defensively. "But I took care of my husband. I take care of my children. It wasn't fair for that man to call me sick and selfish and greedy."

"It wasn't," Fargo agreed as he put on his gunbelt and grabbed up his hat. "I have to go now," he said, stalking toward the door, but he couldn't give up without one last try. He whirled back. "Marion, I really did like it a lot. I like you a lot, too."

"You really mean that?" she asked.

"I do."

Marion Sinclair smiled and then she giggled, bubbling up into giddy merriment. "Bannister told me I was disgusting," she laughed. "He claimed other women never sweat or make noises. I know it's silly, but I got so worried."

"That is silly. In truth, I've never thought much of a horse or a woman who couldn't work up a good lather."

Marion rolled her eyes. "It's a good thing because I'll bet there isn't a good woman around who doesn't get in a lather over you. Including the ones who don't sweat."

Marion quit laughing and gazed at Fargo in that way she had that made him feel as if he was being more admired than any man had a right to be. "I want to thank you, Fargo. For everything."

"It was my pleasure," Fargo informed her, deciding as he did so that it was probably best that he hadn't met her a week earlier. She was the kind of woman who made a man's head swell as readily as his shaft.

"A man who lets flattery go to his head is a fool," Fargo told the Ovaro as he led him out of the stable. "Especially when it's given by a woman who doesn't really give a damn what's inside that head." But flattery did have a way of making a day go better.

* * *

By afternoon, Fargo almost believed that Whitcombe had done him a favor in sending him out to Minnesota. After a pleasant day of riding, he camped by a lake, and the sound of water lapping against the shore lent a sleep-inducing rhythm to the night noises. When Fargo got up the next morning he felt ready to face a whole tribe of amazons.

He spent another pleasurable morning riding through a region rippling and alive with long bluestem grasses. The big bluestem made a handsome carpet, thick and flowered and colorful. The best thing about it was that a man could ride along for hours without getting dust in his eyes. Once he was on reservation land, it didn't take Fargo long to learn the whereabouts of Elizabeth Frasier.

The reservation was home to a considerable number of missionaries and government employees. All were anxious to gossip about the Mrs. Frasier who was deemed a trifle odd by everyone. None of them seemed to know her too well personally, though. In fact, none of them seemed to know much more about her than the bartender in Mankato or the young soldiers at Fort Ridgely.

But they all had stories. Mainly tales about the woman's temper. Apparently, she displayed it quite liberally whenever anybody rode too close to her side of the road or in any way offended her Indians. Everyone seemed to agree that Elizabeth Frasier had her own special group of Indians. They talked as if those Indians were hers, like children belonged to their mother. In truth, most missionaries seemed to make friends just about like everyone else, so they often had special groups of Indian followers. But everybody complained about that trait in Mrs. Frasier.

Fargo hoped it was just professional envy. Maybe they were scared that Mrs. Frasier was racking up too many souls and there wouldn't be any left to save. But as he rode farther onto the Indian lands, Fargo couldn't help but wonder all over again if he really wanted to escort a missionary all the way back to Fort Laramie.

It was a day later when Fargo finally arrived in the squalid settlement in which Elizabeth Frasier lived. Unlike most missionaries, she lived with the Indians, right in the same house, a square ugly brick structure built by the government. There were shacks and sheds and broken farm implements littering a yard where packed dirt patches were the only things hindering a lush crop of weeds, but the acres of just-getting-started corn spreading out in back looked well-tended.

Except for the tepees and the Indians camped in the yard, the place looked like a thousand rundown farms in Kansas and Missouri. Fargo had seen far worse places, but it didn't look like much for a people who had started out with more than twenty million acres of prime land to trade.

The yard held more than a dozen women and children. They hung back, regarding Fargo suspiciously as he dismounted. Most of the women wore plain cotton gowns, although several had wrapped themselves in blankets, as was their custom. The boys were all dressed in brass-buttoned coats with white collars and white man's trousers, and the small girls wore dresses and shifts. From the look of it, the missionaries had been more intent on changing the children's dress than the women's. That stood to reason, since half the children in every Indian camp Fargo had ever been in had run around stark naked in warm weather.

Skye Fargo had just enough Indian blood running in his veins to have seriously considered Bradford's contention that Indians lived better. But he didn't envy these Indians or his Indian ancestors. True freedom was having the option of being a tracker or a shopkeeper, a soldier or a farmer.

Being an Indian child was another matter, though. Indian children were generally wildly overindulged creatures who dashed through the camps, shrieking and laughing and making unholy nuisances of themselves. Their education consisted of endless games of hoops and arrows and playing war and stalking small game.

The children in the yard would have seemed subdued even if they had been white. They clung to their mothers, neither playing with each other nor daring to approach a stranger. All were dark-eyed and somber, but several had hair that caught the sunlight. The sparkling golden high-lights streaking the dark hair framing their small faces gave credence to the charge that the Indian women were being abused by white men. Barton Hughes could deny Elizabeth Frasier's allegations that the women on the reservation were regularly taken advantage of by white men passing through, but at least five of the children in the yard were half-breeds.

Fargo stalked toward the door and the Indians fell back in a wave, parting to let him through. Just as he reached the door an old man came from behind the sheds, shouting.

Fargo turned toward the women. "Any of you understand English?" he asked. From the way they all nervously glanced at each other, he could tell that most of them did. "What's he saying?" Fargo demanded.

The old man was shaking his fist at Fargo and spewing out a stream of incomprehensible words. For several seconds the women were all as silent as stones. Finally one stepped from behind the others. Although pretty, the young woman had more hostility glittering in her dark eyes than Fargo cared to think about. The boy she clutched to her skirts was damned near blond.

"He say you no go in."

"I've come to see Elizabeth Frasier," Fargo told her.

The woman looked at the old man who was still dancing around and shouting. "He know. He say she no want to see you."

"How would she know whether she wants to see me or not until she finds out what I've come for?"

The Indian woman glared at Fargo, not bothering to veil her hatred. "She know. You come from Fort Laramie. She say big chief father send you. Pale sister no want you here."

"Well, since I am here, I'm planning on talking to her," Fargo announced amiably. He took a step toward the door, but the old Indian jumped in front of him with a knife flashing in his grasp. Fargo stiffened. "Tell him I don't want to hurt him," Fargo told the woman without taking his eyes off the old Indian's blade. "But I will if I have to, and he'd better believe I can."

The old man and the young woman exchanged words, too many words as far as Fargo was concerned. He knew they were talking about him. The young woman's eyes kept straying across Fargo. She obviously didn't like him, but Fargo had a feeling she was on his side in this altercation. It was the old man who kept shaking his head adamantly while punctuating his speech by making stabbing gestures with his knife.

"What's he saying?" Fargo interrupted.

"He say you no see Pale Sister," the woman shrugged.

"Well, I'm afraid I'll have to disagree," Fargo said. With quick, fierce movements Fargo used sign language to tell the man to step aside.

Indian sign language was almost universally known throughout the Plains tribes. It was perfectly adequate for communication, although it sometimes left a serious gap in understanding, since many of the signals were accompanied by facial contortions.

Fargo believed a good listener invariably read a speaker's face and his unconscious mannerisms. Those were the things that told you if the man was serious or lying, whether he meant his words or was just stringing you along. Thus Fargo had always felt as if one learned a lot less from someone speaking in sign language—even if the message was exactly the same.

But the medium did have its advantage, especially in displaying a certain degree of ferocity. And the Indians were often impressed by swaggering contentiousness. That was an easy thing to convey by sign.

The old man wasn't impressed, however. He signaled back his "no," as decisively as Fargo had told him to move out of the way.

They were at a standstill. The man was old and lined but proud. He stood right in front of the door, holding the blanket draped around his shoulders in one hand, the knife in the other. He wasn't going to back down. And Fargo was stymied. He hadn't even met Elizabeth Frasier, and already he was caught in a ludicrous predicament. He didn't want to start out by fighting with the Santee.

From what Fargo had heard, that wouldn't endear him

to Mrs. Frasier. The missionary obviously was inside the house and Fargo considered bellowing for her.

Whether she wanted to see him or not, Mrs. Frasier was bound to come out if Fargo made enough noise, but that would give the old man the impression that Fargo feared him. To hide behind the skirts of a woman was a serious breach of Indian etiquette. Just in case Fargo was going to have to deal with the old man in the future, he didn't want to embarrass himself now. Once an Indian put you down, he seldom let you up.

Fargo addressed the young Indian woman. "Go inside and get Mrs. Frasier," he said. "Tell her I'll talk to her outside, but if she doesn't come out I'll break the old man in two."

The woman nodded, then pushed her little boy into the arms of another woman before starting toward the door. The old man protested. He shouted at the young woman. She shouted back.

"He say no," the woman told Fargo. "He say many men come to see Pale Sister. Most men mean. They yell. But yellow-haired bluecoat meanest. Yellow-haired bluecoat come three days past. He hurt Pale Sister. You no see."

"For God's sake, I'm not going to hurt her," Fargo chafed. "Her own father sent me. And if she thinks I'd come all this way without seeing her, she's got another think coming."

"Pale Sister not know Spotted Owl guards her tepee. But yellow-haired bluecoat, he hurt her bad. Maybe Spotted Owl right. Best you no see."

"You don't mean Bannister, do you?" Fargo demanded. "From what I heard, she was the one who got to him."

"Pale Sister make yellow-haired, bluecoat Bannister very mad. But she no hurt Bannister. He hurt."

"Jesus Christ," Fargo swore. "Is the man a fool? Her father's a general."

"Yellow-hair say he hurt friends of Pale Sister if she tell." The young woman lifted her head defiantly, and her black eyes blazed a challenge at Fargo. "We no care. Not let hurt Pale Sister, never again."

Fargo was burning with curiosity about Bannister's transgression. Maybe all that smirking on the part of his men had led him to actually deck a missionary. Anxious to assuage his curiosity and tired of the Mexican standoff, Fargo eyed Spotted Owl.

The old man's attention slipped as the young woman walked back to retrieve her child. Moving like a flash, Fargo dove into the old warrior's side. Spotted Owl staggered and Fargo whirled behind him; his arm shot out and he locked his elbow around the Indian's neck. With his free hand Fargo grasped Spotted Owl's wrist. He twisted and the knife fell on the ground.

"You in the yellow calico," Fargo ordered the shyest-looking of the little girls in the yard. "Pick up that knife."

The little girl stared at Fargo in horror.

"Anna, do what Blackbeard say," the young woman instructed, her hatred a more palpable force than ever as she glared at Fargo.

"Sweet Jesus," Fargo cursed as he watched the little girl creep forward, looking as scared and ready to take flight as a doe facing a hunter. All of the eyes in the yard were turned on Fargo.

These people had a knack for making a white man feel like a villain. An obvious attempt to adapt white customs showed in the women's and children's clothing and even in the little girl's name, but these Indians weren't friendly. All that talk about the Santee being so peaceful was just barely truthful. They were at peace, but they were as hostile as any Indians Fargo had ever encountered. He was damned glad their men were off hunting or fishing somewhere.

"Now hand me the knife, handle first," Fargo directed.

Knife in hand, Fargo shoved the old Indian aside. Then he took a belligerent stance, using the knife to make threatening motions toward the crowd. Fargo didn't draw his Colt, but they were all aware he wore it.

Showing more confidence than he felt, Fargo turned and stepped toward the door. The old man jumped him from behind. But Fargo was ready for it. Grabbing the arm that snaked around his neck, Fargo shrugged to the side, swinging the old man around.

"Get me a rope," he commanded. "Now." Fargo stooped in the dirt, holding Spotted Owl in a hammerlock, and the rope flew out of the air and landed beside them.

"Shit," Fargo muttered as he tied the old man up. "Why is it nobody knows when to give up these days? First a skinny poet. Now an old man. With victories like that, no wonder I feel lower than a snake's belly."

Fargo stood up and dusted off his hands while addressing the crowd in a much louder tone. "Next person who interferes, I shoot," he told them. "I hope you all understand that."

No one tried to stop Fargo as he went inside. The front room was empty of everything, including furniture. There wasn't so much as a curtain in the one small window. It had a sad, barren appearance.

Fargo went on to the back room, where a woman leaned over a pot that was bubbling on the cookstove. Whatever she was cooking, it smelled terrible, like an animal that had crawled in out of the brush to die several weeks ago.

"Excuse me," he said as he wrinkled his nose.

The woman spun around. "Who are you?" she demanded.

"I'm Skye Fargo. I was sent from Fort Laramie to get you. You are Elizabeth Frasier, aren't you?" he asked uncertainly. But he knew she had to be. He'd never come across a woman who came closer to looking him in the eye. She was over six feet tall.

"Yes, I'm Elizabeth Frasier," she answered, looking past him through the door. "Oh, dear God," she cried. "Where is Spotted Owl? He wouldn't have let you come in here alone."

Her spoon hit the floor with a clatter and she rushed past Fargo. He thought about following her, but didn't. Instead he went over to the table and pulled out a chair to sit down on.

"Captain Bannister's amazon," he mused, not quite believing it. "General Colson's ugly daughter." At that he laughed, and it seemed as if he would never be able to quit laughing. Elizabeth Frasier was at least two or three inches over six feet, pretty much on a par with Fargo, but she was willowy and fragile-looking. And without a doubt, she was as beautiful as any woman Fargo had ever seen.

There were ugly women, plain women, pretty women, and beautiful women, but all of them had a tendency to improve considerably when he was in the mood or had had a few drinks. Fargo was cold sober and he wasn't in any kind of mood for improving on things, but Elizabeth Frasier was more like a painting than a real woman. She had very pale skin, but it had a nice pink glow to it. And midnight-black hair that looked dark blue in the light from the window.

Her cheeks had been flushed from leaning over the hot stove, and her eyes had been a wide, worried blue, so blue he would have noticed it a mile away, so blue he was surprised he hadn't felt it before he'd come into the house. The woman had the kind of legendary looks he reserved in the back of his mind for the fair damsel in distress who just might be worth facing a dragon for.

Why hadn't someone told him? he wondered. And then he realized that several people had. There was the more charitable of the missionaries. "I've heard my share of gossip about Elizabeth Frasier," she had said. "But then what would you expect when a woman looks like that? She does stand out in a crowd. Oh, my," the plain woman had clucked, smiling wistfully. "The Lord certainly can be unfair to women when it comes to apportioning looks." He had automatically thought the Lord had cheated Elizabeth Frasier. It kind of changed his viewpoint on the most charitable of the missionaries when he realized the plain woman's sympathy had been for herself.

And there had been the redhead at Fort Ridgely. "She sure is something," he had enthused. "She's awesome." And all the other men had agreed so extravagantly with their nodding and laughing and sniggering that Fargo had assumed that Elizabeth Frasier would be the ugliest woman alive.

"How could you?" Elizabeth Frasier demanded,

storming back into the kitchen. "You left that poor old man in the yard all trussed up like a Thanksgiving turkey."

"Mrs. Frasier," Fargo answered coldly. "That old man pulled a knife on me. And there were twenty people in that yard. All of them agitated beyond reason. If they had decided to rush me, I might have had to shoot. I think Spotted Owl came out all right, considering."

"You would, sir," she countered indignantly. "You were not the one trussed up." Elizabeth Frasier stomped back over to the stove to check on her foul-smelling concoction. Swooping down, she grabbed her spoon up off the floor and thrust it into the pot without even bothering to rinse it.

Fargo wasn't the most fastidious person around, but the floor was covered with dirty footprints, as if all of the Indians had tracked through that morning. Mrs. Frasier picked up two potholders and grasped the sides of the kettle to transfer the steaming pot to the table.

"Need help with that?" Fargo offered.

"No, thank you," she answered.

While Mrs. Frasier stomped around banging cabinet doors and slamming cupboard drawers shut, the stink of the stuff on the opposite end of the table nearly knocked Fargo over. She gathered together a bowl, several crocks of ingredients, some wooden spoons and some measuring cups. Then, not bothering to measure very carefully, she started tossing flour into the bowl.

Elizabeth Frasier was madder than a wet hen and she had a scowl on her that made her brow jut out like rimrock. And still she was as pretty to look at as any sight Fargo had seen in a long while.

8

Skye Fargo stared at Elizabeth Frasier. No matter how hard he tried, he couldn't find anything wrong with her—aside from her personality.

"Doesn't look like Bannister hurt you too bad," he commented.

"Really?" she asked snootily. Her Boston background made the word sound like it might stick in her nose. Or maybe her voice only took on that haughty nasal quality because she had her perfect little nose lifted high so she could shoot Fargo a look that would have withered prairie grass.

"Really," Fargo answered simply.

"And what would you know about it, Mr. Fargo?"

"The folks in the yard mentioned that he hurt you."

"Oh," she mumbled, suddenly looking cautious but a lot less angry. "They shouldn't have said anything. The incident was of little consequence, and quickly forgotten, at least on my part."

Looking down at her batter, she smiled, a bitter but smug little smirk that proved she hadn't forgotten the incident at all. But if Bannister had hurt her, Elizabeth Frasier had at least scored the last hit. Watching her furiously pound the batter she was mixing, Fargo felt his curiosity surge.

"Well, I'm sure your father will take care of Captain Bannister," he told her. "After all, the army can't let its officers go around abusing women."

"My father?" she whispered. Her face drained of color, but almost immediately she fixed Fargo with an angry glare. The color rushed back into her cheeks, a

mottled, patchy rash. "I told you the incident was forgotten," she announced.

Damn, she was pretty. If his curiosity hadn't urged him
first, he might have made her mad only to see her flush.
"You're right, of course," he admitted. "And I'm sure
that as soon as you've told me about it, I'll be able to
forget it, too."

She boiled right up. He could fairly see the steam rising off her as the fire sparkled in her eyes. Her cheeks
were as red as a New Mexico sunset. Her mouth began
to work, and Fargo expected her to erupt like a volcano,
but instead she clamped her mouth shut and lowered her
eyes. She stared so hotly at the batter, Fargo thought it
might cook.

"Have I your word of honor as a gentleman that this
will go no further?"

He gave it.

"Well, it probably isn't worth anything," she commented as she beat her batter savagely.

Knowing he was going to get his way, Fargo laughed.
"Gentleman or not, mine's the only word I've got. So
it's the one you'll have to take. Unless, of course, you
want a full military investigation into this matter."

"You would, wouldn't you?" she huffed as she angrily
swiped back a black curl that had fallen across her face.
"Well, if you must know, Captain Bannister raped me."

Fargo's amusement disappeared entirely as he stared at
her. "Are you sure?" he blurted.

"Yes, Mr. Fargo, I am quite certain," she mocked.
Her hand flew to the buttons of her dress and she flicked
them open impatiently.

"What are you doing?" he demanded.

Elizabeth Frasier tugged the bodice of her dress down.
"I'm showing you," she answered, and the challenge in
her eyes was unmistakable. There was hatred there as
palpable and disquieting as the hatred in the yard.

She was a slender woman, but she was definitely a
woman. Her breasts swelled from beneath an edging of
white lace, and a tiny white bow nestled in her cleavage.
Scratch marks marred her left shoulder. Both her fore-
arms were mottled with purple and red bruises, some of

them clearly fingerprints tipped by the telltale cuts of fingernails piercing her skin. A thin red scratch ran low on her neck, straight across, from the top ridge of her collarbone on one side to the top ridge of her collarbone on the other. She was finely made, her bones looked delicate, her shoulders thin, her neck graceful.

Captain Bannister had obviously held a knife to her throat. Anger welled up in Fargo as he found himself staring at the plump curve of the breast, remembering the cold-eyed, overgroomed captain. He looked away.

"What did you do to him?" Fargo asked, recalling her bitter smile.

"What did I do to him?" she exploded. "I made him angry," she shouted. "But I doubt I made him any angrier than you're making me, and I'm not planning on taking a knife to your throat."

"Mrs. Frasier, you know I didn't mean it that way. You're the one who claimed it was a matter of little consequence. A matter of little consequence?" he fumed. "An incident? I assumed if you could say that, you'd already taken some measure of vengeance."

"Yes," she seethed. "Captain Bannister said he was going to show me my place, but he grew quite negligent afterward. It happened here in the kitchen, and I speared him quite adequately with a fork. I can assure you, Mr. Fargo, that if I had been able to get my hands on a knife, the captain would never have been able to bother another woman, be she willing or not."

"Mrs. Frasier, what Bannister did isn't exactly what I'd call an incident. Don't you think you should do something more about this?"

Fargo looked up again and Elizabeth Frasier's dress was back in place. She had abandoned her mixing bowl and was pacing back and forth with her arms folded across her bosom.

"It isn't what you'd call an incident?" she scoffed. "Mr. Fargo, do you know how often this sort of thing happens on the reservation? Here it is definitely an incident, a quite common one. Captain Bannister says he wants to show me my place. Well, I know my place. We all know our places. Everybody here knows their place. But that doesn't mean any of us like it."

"Mrs. Frasier, you're a white woman. You could successfully press charges."

"A termagant? A hellfire? A woman of poor reputation? A woman who lives openly with savage Indians? Nonsense."

"A general's daughter? A missionary?"

"A missionary? I'm not a missionary."

"Your husband was a preacher."

"Zeke Frasier a preacher? Oh, yes, he claimed to be the Reverend Frasier, among other things. A banker. A doctor. A lawyer. Whatever would serve. Mr. Frasier was an opportunist. And once upon a time he saw an opportunity in a stupid sixteen-year-old girl who was heir to a moderate trust fund through her mother's family."

"Does your father know that?"

"My father," she laughed scornfully. "Does my father know anything about me? After all, I assume he was the one to inform you, and you obviously know very little. But I can assure you, Mr. Fargo, that I cannot go into a courtroom and obtain justice. Nor could I protect the people living here if I were foolish enough to make such an attempt. Unfortunately, Captain Bannister knows my background far better than you and my father do."

"Bannister knew you before you came here?"

"He happened to be present once when my husband was tarred and feathered and run out of a town. That was not an uncommon circumstance. Poor Mr. Frasier. He sold fraudulent stock, nonexistent real estate, unbacked bank notes, and quack medicine, but he was really quite indignant about being caught. He truly believed he had a right to be rich, and that all those mean-spirited, provincial rustics were interfering. And, I must admit, hot tar does burn in the most tender of places."

"If Frasier was that bad, why did you stay with him?"

"He was my husband. I was a stupid child. He was quite handy with a belt. Before six months had passed I'd been arrested on several occasions, ordered out of towns, beaten, humiliated, threatened. There were many reasons I stayed with him for three long years, Mr. Fargo. But none of them were good.''

''How did he die?'' Fargo asked flatly.

Mrs. Frasier halted her pacing and swirled toward Fargo with one eyebrow raised sardonically and humor gleaming in her blue eyes. ''I wish I could say I murdered him. But I didn't. I merely wrote my aunt to say he had passed on, which is quite true. Regrettably, however, there is no chance he passed on to hell. He's out there, someplace,'' she said, waving her hand airily as she resumed her pacing.

''So you're still married to him?''

''Oh, no,'' she denied. ''That's where I was when my father decided to take such an unprecedented interest in me. I was back East, obtaining a divorce.''

Elizabeth Frasier stopped her pacing again to look out the back window. There was nothing out there to see except acres of corn.

''As for my chances against Bannister,'' she said, her back still to Fargo, ''it might help you to know that my husband got everything, my trust fund, my stocks, my jewelry. He wasn't, however, aware that right after we were married I had sent for my mother's jewelry. Ironic, isn't it, that it arrived on the same day he first beat me? I secreted the pieces in a bank vault in New York City at that time. They were still there. I sold them, invested the money, and now receive a very small income. It isn't much, but I share it with these people. They share what they have with me.''

''Mrs. Frasier, your father would be willing to help you if you asked.''

She turned toward Fargo, the fury gleaming in her blue eyes. ''I should humble myself to that man?'' she demanded. ''Haven't I gone through enough? I'm happy here. I understand these people. I know what it's like to have a white man make false promises in order to take everything you've got.''

''Your father wants me to take you to Fort Laramie.''

''I'm not going.''

''You're upset now. We'll talk later.''

''Upset?'' she railed. ''I'm not upset. I am angry and

outraged and absolutely, righteously furious. But I'm in good company. Many of the women here have suffered similar indignities, and the men have been just as thoroughly abased and shamed. Actually, Captain Bannister's action was of very little consequence. He told me to leave, but I'm not leaving. If he thinks I can be so easily defeated, he is sadly mistaken."

Elizabeth Frasier went back to her bowl and threw another cup of flour into the mixture, slinging it down so hard the powder flared up like smoke. The pot she had taken off the stove earlier sat beside the bowl, still stinking to high heaven. Fargo felt sorry for Elizabeth Frasier, but he knew she wouldn't appreciate the sentiment.

He needed some air. Fargo stood up. Then, glancing down into the bowl the woman was working over for the first time, he forgot everything else.

"Goddamn," he blurted. "There's things swimming in there."

"Yes, I know," she said.

"I thought you liked Indians," Fargo chastened.

"Of course I like Indians," she retorted testily.

"Then why would you make them eat that stuff?" Fargo demanded, swallowing uncomfortably as he stared down at a batter full of wriggling white maggots and crawling black weevils.

"I'm not the one who makes them eat this," she answered indignantly. "Mr. Fargo," she added, "I really am quite busy and I don't have time for any more of your questions. I have a great deal to do this afternoon, and you have already wasted much of my morning. Don't you think you should go now?"

Fargo was glad to go. He needed air worse than ever, but he didn't go far. He sat on the ground outside with his back resting on the door. The Indian women and children didn't make him feel comfortable the way they stared, but Fargo thought he'd give Elizabeth Frasier an hour or so to simmer down before he tried to explain to her how her father had become so obsessed with guilt that he was making a dangerous nuisance out of himself. He hoped that telling her how a trip out to Ft. Laramie on her part might spare a lot of people a lot of grief would make her see reason. But he doubted it.

Fargo wasn't even sure there was much reason to it. Elizabeth Frasier had enough problems without worrying about her irrational father and some bedeviled folks at Fort Laramie. But Skye Fargo had been paid well by Whitcombe to care about Fort Laramie's problems, so he had to at least try.

A young boy careened recklessly out of the side yard, driving a small one-horse farm wagon, and Fargo sat up straighter. "What's going on here?" he asked.

Only moments before, the people in the yard had been milling aimlessly around Fargo, trying to make him feel uncomfortable with their stares. Now they nearly tripped over themselves to get away without answering his question. The door behind him opened.

"Mr. Fargo, you are sitting in my doorway," Elizabeth Frasier announced.

"Yep," he agreed, leaning back on the door post to look up at her. She had a baking pan wrapped in a tea towel held out in front of her, a traveling case hanging from her elbow, and a carpet bag slung over her shoulder. "Need some help?" he asked.

"No," she answered curtly.

"Good," he said, smiling. "I didn't really feel like moving."

If looks could kill, Fargo would have been transported straight to Boot Hill. Instead he lounged in the doorway. Bristling, Elizabeth Frasier kicked up her skirts and stepped right over his long, lean legs.

She was perilously overburdened, with the carrying case knocking at her knees, but she had a brisk, no-nonsense stride, regardless. Her flowered blue calico skirts swayed as she walked, swirling around her legs. The little girl in the yellow dress came to the door loaded down with blankets and stopped short, gawking at Fargo.

"Here, honey, I'll take those," Fargo told her. He stood up lazily, easily tucking the child's burden under one of his arms. "Wait," he told her as he shoved his free hand in his pocket and moved to hand her a silver dollar.

She stared at him with dread, her small body trembling. Children liked presents, especially Indian children who came from a culture where there were no prohibitions against begging or accepting gifts from strangers. Indians usually felt that every stranger who crossed their land owed them tribute. Fargo flipped the coin past the child into the living room of the house. "It's yours," he said gruffly. "Go ahead and get it. I'll help Mrs. Frasier."

The little girl wavered for a minute, then wheeled around and ran back into the house.

"Someone sure must have mistreated that child," Fargo commented as he dumped the blankets in the back of the farm wagon.

"Anna?" Elizabeth asked. "Oh, no. She's just started school, that's all. Sometimes it's hard on them. The missionaries mean well, but the second day there Anna drank her soup from the bowl and fished out the meat with her fingers. The next day, she caught her dress on some brambles in the schoolyard, so she took it off. Now she thinks she does everything wrong. She'll get over it." While Fargo retrieved his horse from the hitching post next to the front fence, Elizabeth turned to gaze back at the house where Anna had disappeared.

She turned back to find Fargo tying the Ovaro to the back of her wagon. "What are you doing?" Elizabeth demanded.

"What does it look like I'm doing?" he countered. "By the way, where are we going?"

"We're not going anywhere," she said, flouncing away.

Hiking her skirts up, Elizabeth swung into the wagon. And Fargo climbed up on the other side. "A shame to pack up all this stuff just to sit here in the front yard," he said as he settled beside her on the wooden seat.

Elizabeth Frasier glared at him, but no matter how forbidding she tried to look, that wasn't the way she came off. Her slightly pouting lips were naturally too red, making her look as if she had just been kissed. Her freshly pinned-up hair was already straggling loose. Long, wispy blue-black tendrils fell across her shoulders. She had the look of a woman who had just been tumbled in a hayloft.

Fargo turned away from her and gazed out over the blue-stem on the other side of the road. There was nothing wrong with being attracted to a woman, but somehow what Captain Bannister had done made it feel wrong.

Elizabeth leaned far forward and slapped down the reigns. "Ged-yup," she shouted, starting the horse into a turn in the middle of the road that nearly lurched Fargo onto her lap.

"Whoa, honey," he shouted, grabbing the reins from her. "You're going to turn us over."

"Don't call me honey," Elizabeth chafed as she settled her shoulders against the rough wooden backrest. She made no attempt to recover control of the farm wagon.

"All right, Lizzy," Fargo agreed. "I'll remember that."

Fargo set the wagon on a steady course down the road, and Elizabeth didn't deign to speak to or look at him again. She sat rigidly, scanning the scenery and purposefully ignoring him. Two or three hours later, Fargo decided he had had enough. The road curved right, cutting across prairie in order to parallel the Minnesota River. The water idled below them, a wide but placid stream beneath the bluffs.

"Maybe you'd better tell me where we're going," he complained. "Before we end up somewhere else."

"I would have told you if you had taken a wrong turn," she said calmly, without bothering to look at him.

"Goddamn," he muttered. "Imagine that, you and me traveling along together in the right direction. I wouldn't have believed that was possible."

"What's that supposed to mean?" she snapped.

"It means I came out here from Fort Laramie on an assignment," he said. "I've got nothing to do with Captain Bannister, the traders, or anyone else you've been feuding with. The least you could do is show enough courtesy to listen to what I have to say."

And then, whether she liked it or not, Fargo told her about her father. He told her about a man who was filing reports right and left and disrupting every fort in the West, about a man who wanted to hang a transcendentalist poet and was willing to declare war on the whole

Sioux nation. "So the West is stuck with a demented general, crazed by guilt and running rampant," he concluded. "Now your father has gone on to complete his tour of inspection, but he's given orders that you be taken to Fort Laramie. He wants you there when he gets back. I know that isn't really in his power, but we were all hoping that seeing you might set him straight. Otherwise it's going to take a lot of counter-reports, hearings, nasty maneuvering, and maybe even a court-martial."

Elizabeth nodded, and a small frown furrowed her forehead. "Mr. Fargo," she said. "I'm sure you've heard I'm impossible to get along with, but I am sympathetic. I've fought my share of incompetent government employees, and I know how frustrating it can be. But I can't leave here now. Captain Bannister would think I was running away. I won't do that."

"I guess I understand that," Fargo admitted. "But I don't understand how it all got started. What's your quarrel with Fort Ridgely, anyway?"

"My quarrel isn't with the fort, it's with the system. The traders give credit, then take their money off the top when the government money arrives for the Indians. Since the traders keep the books, the Indians sometimes pay ten times the going rate. The Indians don't have a chance against their duplicity, and they can't survive if it goes on."

"And Bannister?" Fargo asked. "I mean, before he . . ." Fargo broke off. He didn't want to hurt or offend the woman, but he wanted to understand what was going on.

"That's personal," she answered readily, blushing slightly at Fargo's discomfiture but not taking offense. "Captain Bannister's been called in several times to investigate crimes against the Indians, but he never finds evidence. On the other hand, when the charges are against Indians, he's quite efficient. I don't like the man. I never have. But I'm afraid I made that much too clear when he announced he was willing to court me in spite of my dubious background. Willing?" she scorned. "That man told me he was willing."

"I think you're letting Bannister off too easy," Fargo

told her, and his lake-blue eyes narrowed as he studied her.

He couldn't seem to keep his gaze from wandering to where he knew she bore the mark of Bannister's knife, and from there his eyes just seemed to naturally settle on her breasts. Angry with himself, Fargo swung around to glower at the river. "But maybe I could arrange for a private hearing," he offered. "Just between you and me and Bannister."

He glanced back to find Elizabeth Frasier staring at him, her expression more wary and suspicious than any he had ever seen on a woman.

"It's my affair, Mr. Fargo," she told him flatly.

Unfortunately, at that moment Fargo couldn't think about much of anything besides making her affairs his. He kept remembering her yanking down the bodice of her dress, but forgetting what she had been showing him. Instead his mind insisted on musing at the way her breasts had swelled together, hugging at the tiny white bow on her chemise. And under the circumstances that didn't seem very appropriate. Fargo became as rigidly quiet as Elizabeth had been earlier.

They pulled over for the night, and Elizabeth brought out some hard biscuits while Fargo contributed jerky. After seeing her work in the kitchen, Fargo couldn't bring himself to eat her fare, but he helped her unhitch her horse and turn it out to graze. Elizabeth curled up in the back of the farm wagon, and Fargo spread out his bedroll not too far distant.

The next morning they set out again. Neither had much to say, but they traveled along amiably. Most of the day Elizabeth sat on the hard wagon bench, her reflections seeming distant as she studied the countryside. When they stopped to rest and water the horses, the woman offered him a strange combination of tasteless military-style hardtack layered with fairly good strawberry jam—which Fargo accepted gratefully after seeing that it didn't look too bad in the light of day.

If Elizabeth was still roiling with hostility, she was saving it for someone else. She was cordial toward Fargo but cool. Half the time it seemed as if she had forgotten he was along.

It was full dark when they finally pulled into town. In the pitch-black night the last few miles had been harried, and Fargo had suggested they pull over until morning.

"Oh, no, I can't do that," Elizabeth protested. "I have Mr. Myrick's dinner."

An Indian woman opened the door of the house they stopped at, but Elizabeth brushed her aside and bustled into the front room. "Why don't you wait outside?" she urged Fargo as he followed her in.

"Because I don't want to," he answered.

Elizabeth shot him a nasty glance, while the Indian woman merely looked nonplussed as Fargo lounged in the doorway.

"Oh, there you are, Andrew," Elizabeth simpered, addressing the man in shirt sleeves, pants, and stockinged feet who had just emerged from the back room. "I've brought you your dinner." She swept the tea towel off the baking dish with a flourish. "It's a casserole made with all those fine ingredients you sold us. A gift to show our appreciation. Mrs. Myrick, why don't you get your husband a fork?"

The stuff didn't stink so bad now that it was cooked. At least Fargo couldn't smell it from across the room. But he doubted it looked much better. On the other hand, all those critters would be dead instead of wiggling, and that had to be an improvement.

Elizabeth set the baking dish on a wooden table in the corner before she walked back over to the entranceway. With her back to the door, she waited until the Indian woman came out of the back room, carrying a fork that she timidly gave to her husband.

"That's fine, Mrs. Myrick," Elizabeth said. "Why don't you sit down right over there." Elizabeth pointed and the confused Indian woman obeyed. "And you, Andrew. Why don't you taste your food now, before you hurt my feelings? I'm beginning to think you don't like my cooking."

"Is this some kind of a jest, Mrs. Frasier?"

"No," she answered.

And before Fargo realized what she was doing, Elizabeth Frasier pulled a little derringer out of a pocket tucked away in the folds of her skirts.

The trader turned very pale as he stared at Elizabeth, then turned to Fargo. "You're not going to let her do this, are you, mister?"

Fargo was standing less than a foot away from Elizabeth Frasier. He could have easily taken her gun. "Do what?" he said. "She only made you some supper."

"Eat it, Andrew," Elizabeth ordered, waving the derringer.

The trader picked up the dish but balked. "I can't," he whined.

As he wondered how much the black weevils showed in the cooked crust, Fargo wanted a closer look, but he figured it was safer to stay near the door.

"Eat it," Elizabeth commanded. "Now."

The trader took a bite and gagged.

"More," she said.

He took another bite. Elizabeth waved the gun and he took another. Then another. Myrick glanced down at the dish and his eyes grew wide. He started choking.

"More," Elizabeth said.

The trader brought the fork to his mouth, but dropped it as he retched. His vomit spewed into the baking dish. Fargo glanced at Elizabeth, thinking that at this point she would be a little green, too. But she laughed.

"Just a little more, Andrew," she cajoled.

The trader gaped up at her, his face ashen.

"Don't think I won't shoot you," she told him. "Actually, I wanted to. But that wouldn't have been fair. After all, you didn't shoot us. You merely tried to poison us."

"No," he rasped. "It's not my fault if sometimes salt pork goes bad. Or if weevils get in the flour. Usually my merchandise is very good."

"I agree," she said readily. "And I'll be glad to make you another casserole out of the next delivery. But first you'll enjoy this one."

There was a tiny click from the gun and the trader squeezed his eyes shut. He took another bite.

"Let's go," Elizabeth told Fargo.

Fargo drew his Colt. "You go. Start the wagon down the road, but leave my horse. I'll catch up. After all, we wouldn't want Mr. Myrick to believe he had to come after you to show his thanks."

Elizabeth smiled radiantly. "Thank you," she whispered. "I was a little worried about that."

She had never really smiled before, and for a moment Fargo was sure he was in love. But then he turned his attention back to the trader as she slipped out the door. Fargo gave Elizabeth Frasier time to get the slow-moving farm wagon well out of town, and then he followed on his pinto.

9

"I'm sorry, I can't go to Ft. Laramie right now," Elizabeth Frasier persisted.

"I know you don't want to go," Fargo argued. "But Bannister's made a real mess of things. Look, I'll take you out there, where you can wait to see your father. And then I'm sure Whitcombe will see you get back here."

"Oh, hell," she muttered, tossing down her dishrag. Elizabeth left her dishpan and stalked over to the back window. She stood there, staring out at the cornfields.

Her swearing surprised the Trailsman. In spite of her temper, over the past few weeks Fargo had come to think of her as a real, honest-to-God, missionary. She was obsessed by the welfare of her Indians. And she did sleep with them—right in the same room—just like the gossips claimed. The children crowded around her every night, six or eight of them vying to be held in her arms. Some of the other women slept in the empty front room, too. And sometimes one of the men would come in and toss down his blankets.

The house ran informally, its inhabitants coming and going as they saw fit, all of them working when and where they wanted. For the most part, the Indians didn't seem to like the house and thus were seldom in it. Fargo, though, had taken on a rare dislike for the outdoors. Out there everybody glared at him, the men worse than the women.

"Please, Mr. Fargo," Elizabeth pleaded, turning toward him. "You've got to understand. These people almost starved last winter, and now their crop is failing again. The government pays them money once a year. They have no money left from last year, and whatever they accept on credit, they'll pay for ten times over. Their only hope is my small allowance. I'd go with you and wire them the money, but you know they'd be cheated. I can't leave here until the government annuities are paid next month.''

Fargo groaned. The prospect of spending another three or four weeks living with the Indians didn't exactly thrill him. ''All right, then. When the annuities come, we'll go?''

''We'll go,'' she agreed.

''That asshole Bannister,'' Fargo grumbled. ''Can you believe he sent a letter to Fort Laramie complaining about being coerced into dealing with a divorced woman of low reputation who has a lengthy record of arrests? How could he say those things after what he did to you?''

Elizabeth laughed. ''It's all very true,'' she reminded Fargo.

''Well, tell that to your father.''

''I will,'' she asserted, turning back to the window.

''Hey, look, you don't have to do that,'' Fargo objected. ''All you have to do is prove to him you're alive. All anybody wants is to get rid of your father's crazy notion that Whitcombe and I conspired to substitute a dead missionary woman with a paid whore just to influence his insane reports.''

''I am what I am, Mr. Fargo. I'm not ashamed of it. And I don't care what my father thinks.''

Elizabeth Frasier flounced out the back door. In all probability, she had run out to settle another dispute between the children, but it was impossible to keep track of her comings and goings. She was always running around, always doing something. Baby-sitting, dishes, floors, weeding, cooking, anything.

She was the most difficult woman to talk to that Fargo had ever met. He stood, stretched, and ambled over to finish her dishes, certain that he was getting restless when the idea of doing the dishes struck him as entertaining.

Elbow deep in soapy water, Fargo cursed Bannister. Fargo had never seen the letter, but from Whitcombe's correspondence Fargo knew Bannister hadn't presented a very pretty picture of Elizabeth. The picture was so black, in fact, that Colson had decided that the woman Bannister criticized couldn't possibly be the same dear, sweet Elizabeth whom the general could barely remember.

General Colson was getting downright weird. He wasn't even at Ft. Laramie, but he kept wiring everybody in tarnation to protest the fraud he believed Fargo had pulled on him. Half his reasoning was that he believed that if his daughter were truly alive, she would surely have gone to Ft. Laramie to quell the fears of her father.

Whitcombe was now offering twice as much for Elizabeth's return. If Colson kept getting weirder and Elizabeth kept refusing to return, Fargo might be able to retire on what Whitcombe would pay. Even so, it wouldn't be worth the irritation.

Hearing a commotion outside, Fargo went over to look out the window. An Indian he hadn't seen before was standing in the yard, surrounded by the others. One second the stranger was gabbling a mile a minute, and the next he was bent over double with his hands clutched around his middle. But then the Indian did it again and again, talking, then folding, over and over.

Elizabeth came through the back door. "Blue Clay's relatives are sick," she said.

"I could see it was something of the sort," Fargo avowed. "The man's a pretty graphic storyteller."

"I have to go," Elizabeth announced. "I might be gone for a few weeks."

"You just said you couldn't go anywhere right now."

"This is different," she claimed.

"You're damned right it is," Fargo thundered. "You can't risk getting sick now. If you die, your father will be an incurable menace."

"I appreciate your concern for my health, Mr. Fargo," Elizabeth sniffed. "But Blue Clay says that in his brother's camp most of the men are sick, and some of the boys and one small girl. Blue Clay was so frightened he left there almost as soon as he arrived, but one man had already died. It sounds like cholera."

"Let the missionaries take care of it," Fargo proposed. "What good are they anyway if you have to do all their work single-handed?"

"Blue Clay's relatives are Lakota. There aren't any missionaries out there."

There were lots of kinds of Sioux with different habits and different customs—to name a few, the Sissetons, Minneconjou, Brule, Hunkpapa, and Ogallala. The names got pretty complicated since the white settlers, the French trappers, Arapaho, Cheyenne, and the Sioux themselves couldn't always agree on one name for one group. But most folks called the eastern tribes Santee or Dakota, and the western tribes Teton or Lakota. Those in the middle were usually Yankton. Then of course, some Lakota moved east and some Santee west, but on the whole, the Lakota lived out where there weren't as many people. And they weren't nearly as friendly.

"Lakota?" Fargo snapped. "Oh, no, you don't. I haven't gone to all this trouble just to have you get killed. Then your half-baked, harebrained father would be sure I'd cheated him."

"Mr. Fargo, I'm going. I have some matters to attend to first, but I'll be leaving in the morning the day after tomorrow."

"You want to make a bet?"

With her hands on her hips and her eyes flashing lightning, Elizabeth Frasier glared at Fargo. "No, Mr. Fargo," she said coldly. "But if you feel you have enough money for gambling, then kindly donate it to the house fund."

"Goddamn it. A white woman going out there to face cholera and Lakota—just what do you think your chances are?"

"Poor," she pronounced calmly. "But what are those people's chances if it is cholera and I don't go?"

"You can't cure cholera," Fargo blasted.

"No, I can't. But I lived through an epidemic once as a child. I can live through one again. The Indians will panic, though. You know that. They've been decimated by white men's diseases, and they'll be terrified. Blue Clay's terrified."

"Oh, hell. It probably isn't even cholera. I haven't

heard of a major outbreak of cholera in nigh on ten years.''

"Good," she said, already stepping back toward the door. "If it isn't cholera, all I'll have to worry about is the Indians."

"That's all you ever worry about," Fargo shouted after her as she left.

Within the hour Elizabeth Frasier and most of the Indians in the yard had disappeared. The adults left behind were women, six of them. They didn't avoid Fargo, but as they gathered around him in the barren yard their eyes were empty, and their faces were so impassive they might have been carved from stone.

"Tell me where she went," Fargo demanded, and there wasn't so much as a cough, a nod, or a flicker of response in his audience. "You," he said, grabbing the wrist of a woman he knew was conversant in English, "Tell me."

Fargo had been around too long. They weren't even scared of him anymore. He tried signs, gestures, curses, but they were as stubbornly speechless as mules. Finally Fargo threw up his hands and stomped back into the house, harboring a terrible feeling that all of those mute, blank faces were going to burst into laughter the moment he was out of sight.

He glared out the back window, but in actuality the women merely went back to their chores. They didn't even pause to gossip. It was then that Fargo realized the women were worried. They probably didn't judge Elizabeth's chances to be any better than he judged them to be.

Fargo paced until Elizabeth returned late that afternoon. He didn't get two minutes to talk to her, though, since she was followed by a steady stream of missionaries. They arrived bearing piles of old clothes, patched blankets, worn quilts, boxes of jewelry, baubles and beads, lucifers, old silverware, tin plates, whatever they could think of, whatever they could find. Their donations were conspicuously lacking in common food items like flour and sugar, since the Santee didn't have any. It would take a powerful amount of gifts to barter one's way across the Yankton country and into a Lakota camp. Before long the kitchen was overflowing with trade goods and the living room was piling up.

To Fargo's amazement the missionaries were sincere. Whatever personal enmity they felt for Elizabeth was put aside when they considered an illness that sounded suspiciously like cholera, an illness that had already downed twenty warriors and left one dead within twenty-four hours of its onset. Several missionaries offered to accompany Elizabeth, but she turned them down.

On that point Fargo didn't blame her. An army might have helped, but if there was trouble, a passel of missionaries would get in the way. It didn't matter anyway, because Elizabeth Frasier wasn't going anywhere.

A lot of dead Indians was a sad thing, but a dead white woman wouldn't help the situation, and the Lakota were indubitably involved in all the difficulties at Ft. Laramie, along with the Yankton, the Arapaho, the Cheyenne, and the Utes. Most Indians were finding the opportunities presented by half-staffed forts too promising to resist.

The Indians weren't exactly on the warpath, but they were too fractious to tempt, and Fargo couldn't think of anything more tempting than a wagon full of goods traveling with a white woman and a measly two-Indian escort, except maybe a white woman without a wagon full of goods.

There just wasn't a good way for a woman to ride too far into Dakota these days. Quite a few farmers managed it, but the farmers didn't think twice about firing at marauding Indians. Unfortunately, Elizabeth and her emissaries would.

Fargo didn't like her plans, and he wasn't going to let her go. But he let her indulge in her foolhardy preparations. There was no sense in arguing with the woman for two days when a fifteen-minute exchange would serve.

The next morning, the kitchen looked like the site of a rummage bazaar, and the yard like a Missouri livestock sale. A big old Conestoga had been delivered along with all the mules it would take to pull the lumbering monster. In short order the Santee had everything in the kitchen transferred to the wagon.

"You've got to be kidding," Fargo told Elizabeth. "By

127

the time you get out there with that, all twenty of those warriors will be dead.''

"Mr. Fargo, there's nothing I can do for those already afflicted. Certainly you know that. But if it's cholera, I might be able to avert a panic and educate their bereaved companions in methods of treatment.''

"You said a couple of weeks, Mrs. Frasier,'' he countered, emphasizing the form of address the missionaries used, since Fargo had long since taken to calling her Elizabeth, or Lizzy when he wanted to irritate her.

"I've made arrangements for the disposition of my funds with the missionaries. I'm sure my friends here will be fine,'' she assured him blithely.

"And you couldn't make arrangements to go to Fort Laramie?'' he challenged.

"Mr. Fargo, I hardly think the missionaries would be as supportive in regard to my personal business at Fort Laramie,'' she answered arrogantly.

"You're damned right,'' Fargo taunted as she stalked out the back door. ''At Fort Laramie you wouldn't be risking your ass to do their business.''

Fargo wandered out to the yard to inspect the wagon. He couldn't believe so many well-meaning people could be so stupid. The wagon was far too heavy to travel across trackless prairie, but most of the missionaries hadn't been any farther west than Minnesota, which not only had roads but steamboats for the heavy loads.

If Fargo had been willing to let Elizabeth Frasier go out, he would have scotched the whole idea of the heavy wagon and made them pack the mules. But he had decided she wasn't going anywhere except Ft. Laramie. And that was that.

Before dawn on the following morning, the wagon was hitched and many of the missionaries had gathered. The women were hugging Elizabeth and bidding her adieu as if she were a cherished friend rather than the subject of their gossip. Elizabeth had softened under all their fuss, and actually seemed close to tears as she thanked them all—acting like they were doing her a favor by letting her go off to get herself killed.

Fargo lounged in the doorway, watching until Elizabeth climbed up onto the seat. He pulled out his Colt. "Enough of this foolishness," he declared. "Go home," he ordered, aiming his Colt at the group of huddled missionaries. "Or if you want, take your blasted overweight wagon out yourselves, because Elizabeth Frasier isn't going anywhere without me. And I'm not going out there. Elizabeth," he roared, "get down."

From the looks on the faces of all the missionaries and Indians in the front yard, any one of them would have done as Fargo bid, but not Elizabeth.

"I will not," she said haughtily.

Fargo walked over and pulled her from her seat, simultaneously firing at a would-be rescuer. The shot burrowed into the ground, sending up a plume of dust, and everyone stood stalk still, frozen in place.

"Mr. Fargo, you could have killed someone by shooting in such a crowded place," Elizabeth protested.

"Make no mistake, woman," he advised her. "If it's a choice between them and you, they go."

"You—you wouldn't . . . Surely you wouldn't . . ." Elizabeth stammered.

"I would," he corrected, dragging her into the house.

For the first time since he had met her, Elizabeth Frasier looked unsure of herself. She sat down on a chair in the kitchen, staring at Fargo. "But someone has to go. Everything's been arranged. Everything's been packed."

"Let one or two of the missionaries go, then," Fargo suggested. "That's their job. Maybe God will watch over them, maybe He won't. But I'm being paid to watch over you, and you're not going. I told you that at the very first, but you don't listen well."

Elizabeth Frasier nodded dumbly. She sat at the table for fifteen minutes without commenting, and Fargo knew full well she was plotting by the way the blank expression slowly left her face.

But he wasn't particularly worried since he had no intentions of letting her out of his sight again until he left her at Ft. Laramie. If necessary, he would eat with her, sleep with her, even go to the outhouse with her until they were well on their way to the fort. Elizabeth had done him a service in arranging for the welfare of her

Indians while she was gone. Now she had no excuses left not to take a trip.

"Mr. Fargo," she said finally. "I have to see about the wagon and the mules."

"Of course," he agreed, before following her out the front door with the deadly Colt in hand.

The mules were still hitched, the wagon still loaded. The extra stock milled at the sides of the road. Elizabeth addressed one of the Indians as Fargo watched.

"Speak English," Fargo commanded.

"Little Eagle speaks no English," Elizabeth claimed.

Fargo suspected that she was lying, but he had met so many Indians in the last few weeks he couldn't place the one she was speaking to. He let it go.

"Where are the missionaries?" Fargo asked as he scanned the yard.

"They're meeting at the mission school to discuss this situation. They asked that the wagons and mules be left while they try to choose one among them to go. They should make a choice within the hour."

Fargo didn't like having the wagon and mules waiting so close by, but he saw little to remedy the situation. The sooner one of the missionaries left with the wagon, the better. With a resentful glance in Fargo's direction, Elizabeth marched back past him and into the house.

Fargo eased the Colt back into his holster. It was nice dealing with missionaries. He didn't trust them, but he didn't feel he had to watch his back, either. Life seemed a whole lot simpler when the people who didn't like you weren't the sort who would kill you, and Fargo was positive that no one at the house would even consider murder.

The Indians weren't friendly, but they had quit viewing Fargo as a threat to Elizabeth. Since they no longer considered him a threat, Fargo knew they would leave him alone. Although they wouldn't have thought of interfering with her arrangements, Fargo figured from their doleful manner over the last few days that most of the Indians didn't approve of Elizabeth's plans any more than Fargo did.

No, Fargo decided, there were no murderers lurking

nearby. He sat down at the kitchen table and smiled as he recalled unseating Elizabeth. Nowhere else could he have held off forty people with one gun.

"Do you want coffee, Mr. Fargo?" Elizabeth asked coldly.

"Sure," he agreed. It was early. The sky outside the window was still gray-blue with dawn.

Elizabeth pushed a cup in front of Fargo. And then she sat across from him, glowering sullenly as she lifted her own cup to her lips.

"Yuk," Fargo spat.

"I'm afraid I had to add a touch of cinnamon and a good deal of grain to stretch the grounds," she revealed. "We can't really afford much coffee."

Fargo nodded as he sipped the foul brew. It was pretty terrible, but he had already accepted her begrudging hospitality.

"Would you care for more?" she asked when he finished it.

"No," he said decisively.

Elizabeth stayed at the table, staring out the window at the fields of stricken corn. It wasn't like her to sit so long.

"Look, I'm sorry I had to do it," Fargo confessed. "But it was too damned dangerous."

Elizabeth sighed as she turned to face him. She looked tired but beautiful as she glanced down at their empty coffee cups. Her long black lashes were in stark contrast to her pale cheeks.

"I'm sorry, too," she whispered before turning back to study the crop beyond the window. The wilted rows of corn were plainly illuminated by the rising sun.

"Jesus," Fargo gasped five minutes later as he clutched his belly. Elizabeth whirled around in her chair and stared at him with moist blue eyes. "You goddamned bitch," Fargo rasped as he realized the full import of Elizabeth's compassionate expression.

"I am sorry, Mr. Fargo," she announced quietly. "But it will only last a few hours."

Fargo drew the Colt, holding it in his shaking grasp, but Elizabeth ignored it. She knew he wouldn't shoot her. Fargo lurched against the table as she went out the door, but she had beaten him for the time. He staggered to the back door, then ran blindly to the outhouse, the cramps in his belly seizing all his attention.

Feeling as weak as a newborn, Skye Fargo pitched his bedroll in the corner of the living room that night. The Santee gave him a wide berth. In fact, none of them even ventured into the house. Riding out early the next morning, he caught up with Elizabeth that afternoon.

She was still in well traveled territory, making her way up the Minnesota River toward Ft. Abercrombie. Elizabeth shouted something in Sioux to the two Indians who rode alongside the wagon. They backed their horses off, then turned to watch warily as she greeted Fargo with her derringer drawn.

Fargo pulled his pinto up several yards away from the wagon just in case Elizabeth surprised him and did decide to shoot. Women could be unpredictable, but Fargo figured he was safe enough since there wouldn't be any accuracy to her little derringer. He doubted she was much of a shot anyway. He faced her with the Colt.

"If you think that's supposed to scare me," he said, "you might consider that I could kill both of your friends and you before that little whore's gun could take me down."

"Perhaps," she agreed without flinching or balking at all. "But I don't think you would."

She was a damned hard woman to bluff, and Fargo decided right then and there that he would never play poker with her. "I'll make you a deal," he offered. "I'll ride along with you for a few days and tell you all the reasons you shouldn't be out here. Maybe I'll even convince you. If not, we'll have that gunfight on . . . let's say high noon of the third day."

She regarded him speculatively for several minutes. "Tomorrow is the first day, not today?" she asked.

Fargo couldn't really see what difference it made. He thought about it for a minute. With mules, two and a half days would get them seventy-five miles at best, farther

132

than he'd like but not into truly dangerous country. "Sure," he agreed.

The first thing in the morning, Fargo started his project to get Elizabeth to turn back. First he told her about how the wagon was an overweight, lumbering beast not meant to go anywhere off the beaten path. Then he went on to explain how the Sioux were bothering folks around Ft. Laramie. He hadn't figured that would work, but he was ready with an impressive collection of true tales about folks who had been skinned alive, scalped alive, disemboweled, dismembered, raped, starved, tattooed, beaten, spit on, stepped on, ridden on, and carved on.

His recollections carried him through the first day, and he started in again the next morning. Finally Fargo added a few stories about folks who had had their tongues cut off and their eyes plucked out—stories he wasn't quite as sure were true, since he hadn't seen any of those folks personally.

It was a little after noon, and he had talked so much he was hoarse. Little Eagle and Red Wolf took turns driving the wagon while Fargo and Elizabeth strolled along. Being over six feet tall, Fargo couldn't remember having ever walked with a woman who suited his stride and his height so well.

Rather than putting her hair up, Elizabeth had merely tied it back. The black mass tumbled down to her waist. It stirred in the breeze and wisps of it circled around to embrace her slender shoulders. She gazed out at the horizon with eyes as blue and clear as an autumn sky. She looked beautiful, but she didn't look any more perturbed than a porcelain doll would have. Fargo decided his stories were worrying him a lot more than they were her.

"Dammit, you're not listening," he chided.

"Pardon me?" she said, turning toward him.

"You haven't heard a goddamned thing I've said," he complained.

"But I have," she objected. "You were just telling me about a man whose entrails were eaten by Indian camp dogs while he screamed for mercy."

"And that doesn't bother you any?"

"I suppose I'll have to face it if it comes," she answered simply, turning away again to study the horizon.

Elizabeth Frasier paid no attention to him. Never in his life had Fargo met a woman who paid so little attention to him. With all of her comings and goings, and her working here and her running there, Elizabeth had scarcely seemed to notice him. And now with nothing going on, she still didn't notice him. But two could play at that game.

Fargo scanned the land. They had left the river behind early the day before, and the tall green grasses rippled out in every direction. The sky was a mild blue untouched by clouds overhead, but there was a brooding darkness to the west, barely visible but there.

Fargo glanced back over his shoulder. The wagon bumped and lurched about a quarter of a mile back, with the extra mules trailing behind. The white canvas was as bright as sails on the sea, making the Conestoga picturesque even it it wasn't traveling any better than Fargo had predicted. After dropping back to let the horses graze, Red Wolf was catching up. Despite his white man's clothes, he seemed just right with his black hair streaming as he thundered across the prairie, looking for all the world like a triumphant raider making off with Fargo's pinto and Little Eagle's spotted pony.

Fargo glanced back at Elizabeth. She had such a faraway look in her eyes, he doubted she would ever come back on her own. He reached down and plucked a flower from beside the trail. "A flower for your thoughts," he offered.

She flinched, startled, then laughed as she saw the flower. "Did you say it was for my thoughts?" she asked, taking the flower from him.

"Yep."

"I was thinking about the Mandan," she said. "They lived not too far north of here. A tribe of sixteen thousand diminished to thirty-one by smallpox."

"Such pleasant thoughts," Fargo muttered. "I think I'd rather have my flower."

Elizabeth laughed riotously, twirling around as she did so. Her hair whipped across her face and she pushed it back impatiently. ''My thoughts unpleasant?'' she hooted. ''And what about your thoughts? A baby who was held by his feet and swung into a wall until his skull shattered like a melon? A woman split in two because her legs were tied to two separate horses?''

''I was just trying to talk some sense into you,'' he complained. ''But unfortunately you've got more courage than you've got brains.''

''You're wrong,'' she laughed. ''I have no courage whatsoever, but I have very little to lose.''

''That's a terrible thing to say,'' Fargo snapped, swinging in front of Elizabeth and grabbing her by the shoulders. ''You could lose everything. Can't you even try to understand that it's not even unlikely? Chances are, you really will die out here.''

Elizabeth's smile disappeared and her eyes filled with confusion. ''I'm sorry,'' she whispered. ''But Mr. Fargo, you really shouldn't be here. I hadn't meant to endanger your life.''

''Aw shit,'' he growled, letting go of her shoulders and starting back down the trail. ''Can't you quit trying to take care of everyone else. What about your life?''

''I'm doing what I have to do,'' she answered staunchly.

''Bullshit,'' Fargo spat. ''You're throwing it away. Look, don't you want children some day? A husband? A home?''

''No.''

''I think you're kidding yourself. Everyone wants those things. Even I want those things—although admittedly I hope they're a ways off yet.''

''You're wrong,'' she burst, her eyes flashing as she bristled up. This time Elizabeth stepped in front of Fargo. She placed her palm on his shirt front. ''I had a husband, and I don't ever want another one. And as for children,'' she seethed. ''I wouldn't bring children into this world. Children don't understand. When a child is hungry, he sees a piece of bread, and he wants it. He doesn't understand saving it for another day. He cries for it, begs for it, screams for it, and all he gets for his trouble is punished. Then he wonders what he did wrong. 'What did I do wrong, mama? What did I do wrong? I'm hungry. Is it because I stepped on the dog? Is it because I slapped my brother?' '' Elizabeth's words were childlike, but her eyes were alight with anger. "Children always think they can get things by trying harder. They just don't understand."

She whirled away and started down the path once again. Fargo caught up with her, watching as her focus slowly softened on the horizon. The faraway expression settled on her features again.

"Some things aren't so bad," he said quietly. "What about that sunset last night? All streaky pink. The same color as a homemade peppermint stick, but bigger and brighter and one hell of a lot sweeter."

"Oh, for God's sake, Mr. Fargo. You're beginning to sound like a man who keeps poetry in his saddlebags."

"You were in my saddlebags?" he accused.

"You asked me to get your canteen."

"So I did," he admitted sourly.

Turning on him with her hands on her hips, Elizabeth rolled her eyes in exasperation. "Mr. Fargo, you needn't act so embarrassed. After all, I know why you carry Thomas Bradford's poetry with you. Actually, I borrowed it last night. I was curious about the man who had so enraged my father."

"What did you think of him?"

She smiled. "It was a little boring," she confessed. "And a little silly." Her lips twitched before she fell into ribald laughter. "Oh, but when I read it, how I wished I had known the man back in Boston. I surely would have fallen in love."

"With Thomas Bradford?" Fargo blurted, wondering if all the women in the world had gone insane.

"Oh, Mr. Fargo, you're forgetting I don't know him," she laughed. "Is he really that bad? Never mind. I suspect he is. But six years ago, he couldn't have been any worse than I was. I couldn't dance. I couldn't flirt. I couldn't even converse without stammering. But oh, how I could have dreamed about becoming an Indian. Riding bareback. Cleaning hides. Doing beadwork. Putting up tepees. Those things would have sounded splendid after my many social failures.''

"You couldn't have been that bad.''

"In truth, I wasn't. I was merely a pretty girl over six feet tall. But what would you know about such things, Mr. Fargo? I have a feeling you've never been really embarrassed. Never thought you were grotesquely deformed. Never wanted to die of mortification.''

"I suppose I have once or twice. But I was a farm kid. We smoked our cigars behind the barn and sowed our wild oats in the bushes. Life was easy. We all thought we were really doing something.''

"Not all,'' she laughed. ''I'm sure there were awkward farm boys, too. You've just always been perfect.''

"Are you making fun of me, Lizzy?'' he asked, his lake-blue eyes growing serious as he studied her.

"No,'' she murmured. ''I'm just trying to exorcise the ghosts of childhood. It was so terrible. As long as I live, I won't forget the time I was with a boy this tall.'' Elizabeth waved her hand below her neck. ''Before anything untoward happened, I was humiliated. Everyone was looking at the outrageously tall girl I was at sixteen, and the short, rather chubby gentleman who followed her around. As I remember it, he was a Harvard boy, nineteen, rich, considered an outrageously good catch. But I would have gladly thrown him back. What difference did character, breeding, and kindness make when he was so much too small, a veritable minnow?''

Elizabeth sighed and a wistfully sad smile transformed her face. ''We were standing at the refreshment table when the hostess dropped a tray of pastries. The boy gaped. A woman lurched into me, and I fell forward. The world paused for the longest moment while that boy's mouth pressed against me. Afterward, I had a stain on my dress right here,'' Elizabeth said, circling her breast with her forefinger. ''Of drool and pastry. The boy ran off, as mortified as I was. Some of the older women looked shocked, but everyone else was laughing. And I wanted to die. I knew I would die. Perhaps it's silly, but to this day I know I'd prefer to face Lakota than live through that night again.''

Fargo felt Elizabeth was being more than silly, she was being an idiot. Sure, miserable things happened to you when you were a kid, but people grew up. And she had grown up beautifully, but was ready to toss all that beauty away just because she couldn't take the Lakota more seriously than she took a bunch of sniggering socialites.

But before Fargo could comment, Red Wolf rode up and dismounted. He talked to Elizabeth in Sioux.

"Red Wolf and Little Eagle want to go hunting if you have no objection," she translated.

Fargo scanned the prairies. There was a storm far to the west, but no smoke, no dust, no movement otherwise. "No, I don't care."

Fargo drove the mule team another ten miles that day. Elizabeth was quiet again, and the Indians planned to be gone till morning. But Fargo didn't care. He was too busy trying to figure out how he was going to get her to return to the reservation without having to shoot her first. The countryside surrounding them was too empty; it looked like a perfect hunting ground.

The drizzle started right after dinner. Fargo hadn't counted on it, but the solution to his problems was falling from the heavens. The dark blue dusk was laden with heavy black and gray thunderheads. If the storm proved to be as bad as the sky promised, the wagon wasn't going anywhere.

10

The rain poured down, soaking into the canvas over Fargo's head. Small leaks had sprung up everywhere, making the inside of the crowded wagon moist and chilly. Fargo turned to avoid an annoying drip that plagued his sleep, and Elizabeth burrowed back against his warmth. Her ass wriggled into his groin, and Fargo bolted up.

"Mr. Fargo," she whispered. "Is something wrong?"

"I'm going for a walk," he told her gruffly. "I can't sleep in here."

"Wait," she said.

She struck a match and lit the lantern, then hung it on one of the hickory bows that supported the canvas. Water dripped into the flame, making it sizzle and flicker as Elizabeth sank back down into their pile of blankets. Sleepy and disheveled, she gazed up at Fargo. Her blue-black hair tumbled around her, cloaking her white nightdress.

"You can't go out there," she said. "It's raining."

"I know that," he replied irritably. "But I'd rather have the rain pouring on me than have a single drip aiming for my eye socket."

"We could change places," she suggested, scooting over to leave Fargo the narrow space between her and the damp canvas.

"No," he said flatly, turning to leave. He was standing up, but uncomfortably, since he had to bend to accommodate his height.

"Wait," she said.

Fargo swung around and his head grazed the swollen canvas. "Shit," he muttered as his forehead struck one of the supporting bows, and a stream of water splashed onto his face.

"Mr. Fargo, this is ridiculous," she claimed. "You can't go out there. You'll get buried in mud. Surely we can find you a suitable place to sleep."

"I want to go out there," he growled, glaring down at her upturned face. Her cheeks were flushed and her gaze was still soft with sleep. "I need to cool off," he asserted.

"Cool off? But Mr. Fargo, it's positively chilly in here."

"Not with you squirming around the way you do."

"Oh," she murmured, her eyes narrowing thoughtfully as she looked up at him. "We can certainly take care of that. Although I will have to make some preparations first, if that's amenable to you?"

But Fargo merely stared back at her, wondering if she could possibly be suggesting what he thought she was suggesting.

Apparently taking his silence as an affirmative, the woman turned and opened the carpet bag stuffed behind her pillow. Withdrawing a small knitted bag, she dumped out the contents on the blanket next to her while Fargo stared on in fascination. He was vaguely familiar with the items spread out on his bedroll, having glimpsed them on occasion in the top dresser drawers of various women. But he had never seen them put to use. It was the kind of thing a woman ordinarily took care of under cover of darkness, or before she let a man into her room.

Fargo found himself grinning as he concluded that Elizabeth must have noticed him a lot more than he had thought. "I suppose you just happened to have those things along," he commented as she tugged her nightdress up around her thighs, revealing her long slender legs.

"Mr. Fargo." She glanced up at him archly. "You are being obtuse. I thought you might prefer it if I left the lantern on, since these quarters are close and a false move on your part could bring everything down on my head." Elizabeth glowered at the teetering piles of trade goods they had stacked up in their attempt to make room for the bedroll, then turned her gaze back on Fargo. "But you could at least turn your back," she concluded, "since even the lowliest crib girl is entitled to some privacy."

"And what would you know about crib girls?" he laughed, readily turning away since he didn't want to risk having her turn off the lantern. There were things about Elizabeth that Fargo definitely was interested in studying up close, under good light, things a lot more attractive than her contraceptive paraphernalia.

"Mr. Fargo, I think it's only fair to tell you that I am very well acquainted with most facets of whoring. And as for my pharmaceuticals—I am traveling with three men into a camp of warriors. It would have been remiss of me to not take some precautions. Considering the circumstances under which we met, I'm afraid you may have misunderstood my position. I'm not a missionary, Mr. Fargo. On the contrary, I'm not only jaded enough to consider copulation a fact of life, I'm also experienced enough to guard against pregnancy and disease."

Fargo's assumption—that Elizabeth had actually noticed him after all—exploded, and he was left feeling as if she had knocked the stuffing out of him. "Are you trying to tell me you expect to be paid for your services?" he asked, turning back to find she looked just as beautiful even though he felt considerably less enthused. Her paraphernalia had been safely tucked away, but her nightgown rode high on her thighs, giving him plenty to look at.

"Good heavens, no," she gasped. "I only wanted to keep you from misconstruing the situation."

"Which is?" Fargo asked, not at all sure what was going on between them. It certainly didn't remind him of any situations he had ever gotten involved in before.

"Pardon me?" she said, looking dumbfounded.

"Just what in hell is our situation?"

"Well," she said uncertainly. "You're a man. I'm a woman. We need rest, but you couldn't sleep and I saw no reason for you to be uncomfortable or muddy. I suppose it's as simple as that."

"You mean you'll fuck me so I won't get wet?"

Elizabeth licked at her pouty red lips nervously. "Is

there something wrong with that?" she asked hesitantly. "I mean . . . Well, I'm sorry if I offended your moral sensibilities."

Fargo shook his head as he started to unbutton his shirt. "Hell, no, there's nothing wrong with that," he admitted. Although he sure wished she would act as if he had something to do with her offer. Elizabeth made him feel as if she would have made the same decision if he had been a hunchbacked, bow-legged, drooling old reprobate. "Well, let's get to it," he said, after stripping his pants off and kicking them aside. "After all, time's a wasting, and we need our rest."

"Of course," she murmured. She looked a little upset but no more upset than Fargo felt. "Do you want me to take this off?" She clutched the front of her nightgown.

"Sure, why not? After all, it might get in the way and slow us down," he baited.

Elizabeth tossed her nightdress in the corner, then sat on the bedroll with her arms wrapped protectively across her breasts. Her black hair fell across her white flesh. The bruises Bannister had inflicted were gone, but her bones looked as fragile as ever. She was trembling and there was a hint of fear in her eyes. "I have offended you, haven't I?" she whispered.

"No," Fargo answered, suddenly not feeling at all offended.

"Good," she said as she eased down on the bedroll. Turning her face to the canvas wall, Elizabeth drew up her knees and spread her legs.

"Jesus," Fargo muttered. "Don't you think we should at least take a minute to get acquainted?"

"Please, Mr. Fargo," she said. "Can't we just get this over with? I don't know why, but you're making me exceedingly nervous."

"Over with?" he bellowed, feeling so insulted that he was tempted to tell her where to go, until he admitted to himself that he really didn't want her to go anywhere. "All right," he said as he dropped onto his knees between her legs. Fargo stared at her firm, flat belly, at her delicately arching pelvic bones, and at the swath of midnight-black hair nestling between her thighs, but she was waiting.

He thrust into her. She was hot and dry inside—not much more soothing than a piece of sandpaper. But worse, she kept her eyes squeezed shut and her face turned to the canvas.

"Goddamn it," Fargo mumbled, pushing himself up over Elizabeth to grab her shoulders. "Couldn't you at least pretend you like me?"

Elizabeth jerked her head around to glare at Fargo. "I don't pretend," she hissed.

"Some whore you must have been," he sneered. "You think you're doing me a favor, don't you, Miss High-and-Mighty? But the mud outside would be more gratifying. Do you know what you feel like?" he demanded, thrusting down hard to taunt her. "You're like a dried-up old spinster. And you're stiffer than a corpse."

Elizabeth glared blue fire at him. There was hate in her eyes, hate as glowing and hot as flame. "I won't pretend," she seethed. "Not for anyone. Not anymore. But you're wrong, Mr. Fargo, I was a good whore. I was a good whore because my husband made me pretend while he sat in his closet—monitoring. My husband who complained that I moaned more for handsome men, that I made the bedsprings squeak louder for tall men, that I screamed more for well hung men."

Fargo stared at the woman. She looked like something out of a fairy tale—Snow White brought to life, the fairest of them all—but all he could find in her blue eyes was hate.

"Zeke was always reminding me that all of the men paid the same amount and should receive the same treatment," she snarled through clenched teeth. "He made me moan for all of them, beg for all of them, pant for all of them, scream for all of them. Or be beaten. It was my choice. But I'm not frightened anymore, Mr. Fargo, and I won't pretend for anyone ever again."

"What's wrong with you?" Fargo demanded, awed by the hate that glittered in her eyes. "I didn't ask you to crawl in bed with me. I didn't ask you to do anything. This was your idea, not mine. So you can just quit acting like I'm Bannister or your husband because I haven't done anything to you."

"Are you really so different?" she jeered. "What do you care? You don't even like me, Mr. Fargo. You're no different from the others. You take what you want, and to hell with the rest. My husband wanted money, and you want . . . ?" Elizabeth laughed but the sound was distinctly unpleasant.

"What is it with you?" Fargo shouted. "Do you think other people don't hate? Unlike you, I was a happy kid—until my folks were murdered. I hated the men who did it, I still hate them, but I wouldn't take it out on you. I don't throw it at just anyone. Why can't you hate your husband, Mrs. Frasier, and leave it at that?"

Abruptly Fargo realized he was shaking the woman's shoulders and shouting at her. Gently he pushed the dark hair away from her pale face. "Or have I hurt you somehow?" he asked.

"No," she denied as the fury faded from her eyes, until she looked frightened and vulnerable.

"Oh, hell," Fargo murmured. "It isn't fair. You're the most beautiful woman I've ever seen. You've got more fire in your eyes than most people have in their souls. And you can put more passion into a fight than most women will ever know. Goddamn, I thought this was going to be a night to remember." Fargo laughed lowly. "Well, come to think of it, I guess you have made it that."

Fargo didn't have any idea what he was supposed to do, but he didn't feel much like finishing what he had begun. Sighing, he rolled off her. He settled back down in the bedroll with his back toward Elizabeth. And the old, agonizing drip found his eye socket almost immediately.

"Do you want me to turn off the lantern?" he asked.

"No," she whispered. Elizabeth sat up and leaned over him. She rested her hand on his bare forearm and her hair tumbled across his face. "Mr. Fargo," she said, but then she paused for what seemed to be forever.

"My aunt and uncle had six grown children of their own when they took me in, and numerous grandchildren

144

visiting daily. My father had always ignored me. Zeke Frasier was the first person who ever really seemed to notice me. My husband was a silver-haired, silver-tongued man,'' she announced quietly. "Even after I knew what he truly was, I did whatever he told me to, because I was terrified he would leave me. And that made me ashamed,'' she confessed. Elizabeth's hold tightened on Fargo's bicep.

"Before long, I pretended that every man was a fond and faithful lover, and that each and every encounter was a beautiful experience. And that made me ashamed. After a while, I only fantasized about the handsomest of the men. And that made me even more ashamed.''

Elizabeth sighed, and Fargo rolled over to look at her.

"My husband used me, he sold me, he beat me, and then he took everything I had left by telling a judge about all the men I'd been with. Zeke chose strange and terrible details. He told the judge about rescuing me from a bed after I'd been left naked with my ankles tied to the posts. He said he had found me once spread out on a sticky sheet, drenched in honey while a short, little man licked the sweet syrup from between my thighs. He told the judge he had once found me on a faro table giving my body to all the players, right there, in plain sight—gambling my body against their winnings.''

There were tears running down Elizabeth's cheeks, and Fargo wished she would stop talking. Her memories reminded him of Bradford's stomach-turning diatribes. But instead of making him feel queasy, Elizabeth made Fargo want her. And that feeling was making him real uncomfortable.

"It wasn't true that Zeke had found me with those men, of course. But the details were true, and I was too humiliated to tell a stranger that Zeke had brought those men to me. I just couldn't bring myself to tell the judge about the closet and Zeke's instructions.''

Elizabeth's story made Fargo think about Bradford and Bannister, two men he didn't want to think about. And it made him think too much about sex, something he felt it best not to think about, under the circumstances. Fargo felt sorry for Elizabeth, but he didn't see that there was anything he could do about her life.

"I lied to you when I said I didn't pretend," she said softly. "My whole life is a pretense. Even now. I pretend I hated all of it. But when Zeke was flush, he was exciting and charming. I pretend I hated all of the men. But day by day, sometimes it was good; sometimes it was awful. And I loved the travel, San Francisco, New Orleans, St. Louis. And that's the worst thing of all. That's what makes me so ashamed. Mr. Fargo, would you tell me that you like me?" she asked abruptly, gripping his arm.

"Well, of course, I like you," he said gruffly, wishing it wasn't quite so true. Wishing that her hair wasn't tangled around him. Wishing that he could just jump up and go out in the rain to cool off without hurting her.

"You're not just pretending?" she whispered.

"Why in hell would I do that?" he challenged. He knew he was getting irritable, but the woman was impossible. She kept leaning over him with her breasts not six inches from his face. Her pink nipples stuck out, tempting him like tasty bits of candy.

"The truth is, you make me furious. You make me crazy, and you fight with me all the time," Fargo ground out. "And you poisoned me," he reminded her. "You can't forget that. But I suppose you've got some redeeming values," he admitted. "And I like you, all right? So why don't you just roll over and go to sleep before I get really mad?"

Elizabeth smiled. "Because I saw you, and I wanted you," she said fervently. "But I was so ashamed I tried to pretend it wasn't happening. I tried to pretend to myself that I couldn't want a man ever again. Not anymore." Elizabeth laughed as she tumbled over him. She rubbed her damp cheek against Fargo's beard. "But I think maybe there isn't any shame in making love to a man who likes you," she murmured, throwing her arms around Fargo's shoulders.

She clung to him, pressing her breasts against him and squirming closer until he felt she had crawled right under his skin. "You do realize that this doesn't make any difference, that I still have to go to the Lakota?" she asked.

146

Fargo nodded. "I know," he sighed as he slid his hands down along the curve of her bottom. "We have a duel scheduled for tomorrow."

"But I do like you," she claimed. "I can't quit fighting. I don't even know how to quit fighting, but I do like you."

And then Elizabeth made love to him. There wasn't any other way to put it. Fargo had a feeling she took all the frustrated love inside of her and poured it all over him as passionately as she vented her anger on him. She wrapped him in emotion.

Her body pressing against him was tense and quivering, and the embrace of her arms was tight and trembling. She smoldered like a banked fire, her movements slow and deliberate but heated. And Fargo let himself fall into it, not giving a damn if he got burned.

The next morning, Fargo awoke to the smell of a campfire. He stretched lazily, remembering the previous night, and then he laughed as he recalled how frustrated he had been thinking that Elizabeth would never get around to noticing him. Hoping breakfast was waiting, he bounded up, got dressed and went outside. Anger started welling up in him as soon as he scanned the camp.

The wagon was bogged down in mud, and the hobbled mules grazed placidly nearby. But the fire was splashed with water to make it smoke. Fargo circled the campsite, getting down on his knees several times to inspect the tracks. Standing, he gazed out over the endless grassland, but there was nothing in sight.

It wasn't hard for the Trailsman to see that Elizabeth had planned her own escape. The fire had been set a couple of hours before dawn, tended until the coals were glowing, then dampened. A nice touch. By the tracks, he could tell the woman had saddled a horse on the other side of the wagon. If Fargo had been alarmed by Elizabeth's early morning noises, chances were he would have turned toward the smoking fire first. So with any luck Elizabeth could have maintained an innocent facade.

And when Fargo had gotten up, the fire had provided a familiar setting. It had kept him from jumping right up and checking on the woman. Elizabeth had bought herself about three hours, and that would be enough.

"That goddamn bitch stole my horse," Fargo roared. But there was nobody out there to hear except the mules, and they didn't seem to care.

Hastily throwing together a makeshift pack, Fargo picked out the sleekest of the mules to follow Elizabeth, but he knew full well that the mule would never catch up to his pinto. Not only was Elizabeth Frasier going to get herself killed, his Ovaro was going to end up an Indian pony.

Two miles out of camp, Fargo found the spot where Elizabeth had rendezvoused with Red Wolf and Little Eagle. Elizabeth had made off with Fargo's horse, his saddle, and his rifle. That left him with his Colt, his clothes, and the knife he carried in his boot. It didn't take much calculation for the Trailsman to conclude that the woman had stolen half of everything he owned.

11

Five days later, Fargo was thrust on the ground in front of a red-painted council tent sitting square in the middle of a Lakota village. Glaring at his husky, bronze-skinned captor, Fargo stood up and brushed himself off. He was a little worse for wear, after having been clobbered in the stomach with a head club and hit over the head with a coup stick, pounded on with an iron kettle, and stuck full of porcupine embroidery quills, but he still had his scalp, and that wasn't faring too badly for someone who'd been caught sneaking around a Lakota camp.

Fargo's pride was a little ruffled at having been discovered by a bevy of shrieking squaws, but he was alive. Actually, he had done pretty well until the camp dogs had betrayed him. A village of tepees surrounded by open country on every side, the Sioux camp was huddled alongside a wide, sandy stream that didn't even boast cottonwoods or willows to shade its banks. Or to hide an intruder. Fargo had never really had a chance, but he had tried. Now he was surrounded by irate warriors smack in the middle of a Lakota camp, and all he could do was hope Elizabeth Frasier had managed a miracle and saved every one of them from cholera.

Just then, Elizabeth showed up. She was being dragged along by a big, brawny, hatchet-faced warrior, and Fargo could tell by the way the man was treating her that she wasn't the camp heroine. It was a disappointment, but on the other hand, Fargo felt relief wash over him just at seeing the woman alive. Since Elizabeth had a lot to answer for, Fargo was trying to stifle his feeling of joy, when, to his amazement, the woman swung around in front of the warrior accompanying her, and started to scream at the man in an unintelligible barrage of Sioux.

Elizabeth stomped her foot and waved her fist. The Indian grabbed her shoulders, and she brought her knee up, landing it solidly in the warrior's groin. Howling, he brought his fist back to strike her, but Elizabeth flew at him, her fingernails clawing his face. Somehow Elizabeth knocked the warrior down and they rolled in the dusty earth, landing only a few feet away from Fargo.

A noisy, jostling crowd was gathering, a crowd of shouting men, shrill women, shoving children, and barking dogs. The whole camp was breaking into pandemonium. And Fargo studied the riotous Indians, trying to see a way to take advantage of the situation. But the mob was closing around Fargo and the fighters in a solid circle.

For the first time Fargo saw what had so awed the soldiers at Fort Ridgely. Elizabeth fought like a cornered weasel, a supple, twisting, slashing spectacle of teeth and claws. In spite of the warrior's bulk, she was holding her own.

She wore a buckskin dress without a blessed thing on underneath, and it had ridden up around her waist, but modesty didn't deter her. Elizabeth didn't seem in the least concerned that she was flashing her scenery at half the village. She had the warrior all tangled up, with her slender, white legs wrapped around his as she clutched him in her embrace, holding on close so he couldn't get any leverage for a blow.

He was yanking her long braids, trying to pull her off, when she clamped her teeth on his jugular. Gagging, he rolled, landing on top of her, but Elizabeth's fingers went straight for his eyes. He lurched back, and she twisted sideways, half of her torso escaping from under his weight.

Even though he feared the punishment might be worse for Elizabeth if he did, Fargo was considering intervening before she got hurt. But before he moved, an authoritative-looking Indian broke through the crowd. He was followed by two warriors wearing unusually dyed buckskin shirts that seemed to be a kind of uniform. Fargo figured they were tribal leaders of some sort. The lead Indian grabbed Elizabeth's warrior by the hair and pulled him to his feet.

The other two Indians dealt with Elizabeth, which wasn't nearly as easy. One on each side, they held her by the arms while she tried to flail loose. The fight was over, but Elizabeth kept screaming at her opponent, and the man kept shouting back. The Indian whom Fargo took to be a chief shouted at both of the brawlers. Then, letting go of his charge, he turned to the crowd and shouted at them, shaking his fist until they started to disperse.

Finding himself free, Elizabeth's Indian came right at Fargo, jabbering and pointing to Elizabeth as he drew his fingers across his neck in an unmistakable gesture. Although Fargo wasn't quite sure whether it was Elizabeth's throat or his own that the man wanted to slit.

A long, lean, bearded white man surrounded by hostile Sioux, Fargo bristled, trying his damnedest to look formidable. It must have had some effect because another uniformed Indian came up and slammed him in the belly with a rifle stock. Fargo doubled over, and Elizabeth's Indian thrust into him, pushing him to the ground.

When Fargo sat up, three rifle barrels were trained on his chest, and Elizabeth was thrown at him. She landed on her stomach in a sprawl across his lap, but she didn't have any intention of staying there. Elizabeth twisted around, all ready to jump back into the fray, and Fargo grabbed her.

"What's going on here?" he demanded.

Elizabeth was panting, her cheeks were flaming, her dress was disordered, and there was dirt on one side of her face, but she didn't seem to be hurt.

"What are you doing here, Mr. Fargo?" she rasped, ignoring his question.

"You took my horse, remember? I followed you."

"I took your horse so you wouldn't follow me," she said indignantly. "A horse is not worth risking your life over."

"That's easy for you to say, it wasn't your horse—until you stole it. Besides, just maybe I came here looking for a woman, although, of course, you wouldn't have thought of that," he reproached her. "Just what kind of man do you think I am, Lizzy?" he asked tightly. "Did you really think I'd turn back without knowing what had happened to you?"

Elizabeth stared at him in confusion. She shivered, and Fargo realized the woman used anger to keep her fear in check. It wasn't a bad technique. He had used it a time or two himself.

Elizabeth and Fargo were sitting on the ground a few yards to the side of the red council lodge with three rifles aimed at them. The warriors were gathering not ten yards away when Elizabeth's Indian broke through the guards and started railing at Fargo all over again. The chief and several of the council members ran over and started yelling at the Indian, but he just kept shaking his fist at Fargo and ranting until finally one of the armed guards whacked the man in the shoulder with a rifle butt. Apparently arrested, the hostile Indian glared back at Fargo as two men dragged him away.

"That man doesn't like me," Fargo commented.

"If it's any consolation, he doesn't like me either," Elizabeth said, staring sullenly at the departing warrior as she played with one of her braids, nervously wrapping and unwrapping it around her hand.

"What was he saying?"

"He thinks I'm your wife."

"And he has designs on you?" Fargo asked.

"Not anymore," Elizabeth sighed. "I'm afraid Tall Tree was berating you for not training me better." She smiled self-deprecatingly. "Married one day, divorced the next. That seems to be the fate of my life."

"You were married to him?" Fargo blurted, staring at her.

"I was given to him. But I think that's about the same thing around here, since I doubt they believe in fancy weddings for captive women. On the other hand, they do seem to think captive women should act like good little wives."

"Jesus," Fargo muttered. "And I thought Belle got herself into fixes."

Elizabeth's eyes narrowed as she studied Fargo. "It wasn't all my fault," she protested. "I tried to be diplomatic and cooperate with these people. But Tall Tree didn't like my cooking, and he spit stew right in my face."

"Not a bright idea, knowing you."

"Well, it wasn't a very happy honeymoon," she admitted.

"I can imagine," Fargo said, trying not to laugh. He lifted Elizabeth's chin and brushed off her cheek. "Elizabeth, are you all right?" he asked seriously.

She pulled her chin away to watch as the Indians filed into the council lodge. "I'm fine," she claimed. "But I wish you hadn't come here."

"Little Eagle and Red Wolf," Fargo said, seeing the two Santee join the other Indians.

Elizabeth nodded. "They'll be allowed to speak, but I'm not sure they can help."

"What happened to the cholera?" Fargo asked, realizing that none of the Indians seemed sick.

Elizabeth didn't look at Fargo as she started chewing nervously at the braid she'd been fooling with. "It wasn't cholera," she said quietly. "It was whiskey. Two warriors and a small girl who had merely tasted the brew died of it. Apparently, some trader thought it would be a colossal joke to lace his wares with a very strong purgative."

"It seems someone shares your sense of humor," Fargo said.

Clutching her braid, Elizabeth swung her head around and gaped at Fargo. "Oh, God," she gasped. "I'm so sorry, Mr. Fargo."

Fargo had to admit that Elizabeth Frasier had been holding up real well for a woman caught in such trying circumstances, but he could tell she was about to break down. He grabbed her braid out of her hand. "Now quit that," he ordered. "I like your hair, and I sure as hell don't want to see it all chewed off."

Elizabeth nodded, recovering a little before she threw her arms around Fargo and held him close. "I'm afraid they're not very happy with white men right now," she whispered. "I think they want revenge for the villainy of that trader, and oh, Mr. Fargo, I'm so afraid any white man will do." Elizabeth clung to Fargo, with her whole body quivering against his as she cried her fears out on his shoulder.

12

The prairie was covered with blankets and quilts. Braves joined their women in frolicking with bonnets and hair ribbons while children squabbled over everything from tin plates to wooden spoons. Two old men disputed a bolt of flannel, ignoring the tumult from the young men who grappled for the same box of baubles.

Lakota scouts had found the wagon Fargo had abandoned and brought the goods in. Everyone in the village—even the tribal council—dropped everything when the travoises arrived. Fargo and Elizabeth were forgotten as the Lakota pawed through the goods assembled by the reservation missionaries.

Now only one guard watched the white captives, and he didn't look pleased about staying on the job. He got more disgruntled every time he glanced over and saw his friends sporting with tinware forks and shiny mirrors. To avoid frustration, he finally herded Fargo and Elizabeth back into camp, then into a tepee.

Glee surged through Fargo. The trade goods had saved them after all. He and Elizabeth sat side by side. The guard squatted across from them, pointing an old Leman trade rifle.

When he peeked out the door, the Trailsman saw their chance. "Cry," Fargo whispered urgently to Elizabeth. The guard instantly turned and shouted at them. "Get hysterical," Fargo ordered, and the guard barked fiercely.

Their ruse worked. Elizabeth began crying in response to the guard's harsh commands. Fargo leaned over her. "Lie down, Lizzy. That's right," he whispered. She threw herself down and launched into a fresh bout of bawling. "Just lie down and keep low."

Fargo stood and the guard's rifle rose with him while the guard shouted. Gesturing toward a heavy buffalo robe nearby, Fargo used sign language to explain that Elizabeth needed comforting. It wasn't helping her to lie on the bare earth. Just then she released a wailing lamentation that any man would want to quell. The surly guard nodded and pointed to the robe.

As Fargo leaned to fetch it, Elizabeth squealed. The Trailsman straightened and flung the robe into the guard's face. The startled Indian's cocked rifle fell silently onto the dirt.

Fargo couldn't believe their luck. He had expected the old Leman to discharge and alarm the entire village. He had been gambling that the shot wouldn't hit anything and that they might get away in time.

Before their guard could get out from under the buffalo skin, Fargo flew at the warrior. Elizabeth dived into the fight. While Fargo struggled with the hooded guard, trying to wrap him up, she clubbed the Indian with a frying pan.

"You know, you're not too bad in a fight," Fargo commented as he grabbed Elizabeth's wrist and headed for the door flap. "Maybe I should take you along on more of my jobs."

He looked up. "Shit."

Tall Tree stood in the entrance with four friends behind him. The bare-chested Indian wasn't nearly as tall as Fargo, but he was brawny. He wore a breechcloth, leggings, and moccasins, with his thick braids wrapped in fur. He looked every inch a Sioux warrior, but he pointed a Navy Colt.

Tall Tree issued brusque commands, and Fargo raised his hands and backed off. "What's he saying?" Fargo asked.

Elizabeth sighed. "He says no woman will make a fool of him without paying."

"I thought he was under arrest," Fargo complained.

"Mr. Fargo, I don't think they have rules against fighting with captives. He was merely detained in order to keep him from interrupting their council meeting."

Fargo grimaced, his spirits sinking as the five warriors

stepped into the tent. Two grabbed Elizabeth. Fargo stepped forward. A third swung a hammerlike club tipped with a big, oval stone. Fargo dodged in time to keep his brain from getting scrambled but not in time to avoid the blow entirely.

When he came to, the faint and nauseated Trailsman felt mildly surprised to be alive. His shoulders ached, his belly churned, and his head pounded. It didn't help a bit that the Indians were whooping and howling. They were close by, almost within reach, he figured. Trying to collect his thoughts, Fargo lay still. Perhaps the Indians thought he was dead, and he didn't want them to think otherwise for a while.

Amid the din he listened for sounds of Elizabeth. Finally there was a sobbing intake of breath. She wasn't the type to scream or cry, but from the other sounds he deduced the Indians weren't treating her well. He tried to ignore their grunts, hoots, and catcalls so he could clear his head. Until that happened, he couldn't help himself, much less her.

He slowly opened his eyes. He saw only whirling black specks and somersaulting rainbows at first, but his vision slowly focused. The Lakota had kicked him to the inside rim of a tepee, where the wall had been rolled up a foot or so for ventilation. This was a big tepee, big enough to leave him some room at the perimeter between the cluster of warriors in the middle and the external ring of poles that formed its conical framework.

Not really wanting to see what the warriors were doing with Elizabeth, Fargo turned his head just enough to tell whether anybody was watching him.

Nobody was. Those nearest had their backs turned while they stomped and hollered to encourage the warrior currently bouncing atop the white woman. Those on the other side, who might have noticed Fargo if they moved their heads, were too intent on the show. Fargo caught a glimpse of pale flesh before he turned away.

Speed and silence were tough when a man had to crawfish through the litter of a camp, especially when every silent breath hammered viciously at his belly. But the camp was empty. Except for the warriors in the tepee, everybody else was still out on the prairie, enjoying the trade goods. Fargo slithered under the rolled-up wall and got behind the tepee. He was just getting his feet under him when a hand gripped his shoulder. Frustration ripped through him. It was all he could do to keep from shouting his anger.

"Mr. Fargo," a voice whispered. It was Little Eagle, the Indian Elizabeth had claimed spoke no English. "Red Wolf waits with the horses outside the village."

"My Ovaro?" Fargo rasped.

"Your horse."

To Fargo's astonishment, Little Eagle handed him his Colt, which had been confiscated when he was caught. "Can you get some rope?" Fargo asked. "A lot of it."

The Trailsman sprawled on the ground, gulping fresh air until Little Eagle returned moments later. The warriors were still occupied with Elizabeth, and the rest of the village remained out on the prairie, enjoying their newfound wealth. Fargo rose to start stealing three convenient horses. Since Indians picketed only their best mounts inside their villages, he quickly found three ponies that weren't quite as scraggly as the usual Indian stock.

Roping a tepee top turned out to be more tricky than Fargo had supposed. But the men inside made enough noise to cover his first four failures. The plan seemed safer than taking on five men with the Colt, since any one of them might decide to use Elizabeth as a shield. His fifth toss caught; Fargo backed the stolen pony until the rope was no longer slack.

After signaling Little Eagle, Fargo prodded his pony. The braided rawhide rope from the horse to the tent grew taut. Abruptly the tepee came over. Poles rained down until the hide cover began to billow. Braves struggled to escape the falling canopy, only to get whacked by errant poles. As soon as they could get free, they scattered. Scurrying like rabbits, they kept their arms up over their heads for protection from whatever else might fall on them.

Leaping from his pony, Little Eagle kicked aside the stunned brave who still straddled Elizabeth. While she and the Santee sprinted to their waiting horses, the first wave of villagers appeared from beyond a tepee.

Little Eagle helped Elizabeth mount, and the three ponies careened through the camp, Fargo's still trailing several poles and the huge tepee cover. Fargo turned to ride straight toward the main horse herd; Little Eagle and Elizabeth followed. As they rode past the last tepee, Red Wolf joined them, leading Fargo's Ovaro and two other saddled horses.

They stampeded plenty of Indian horses before Fargo cut the rope that dragged the tepee cover. But bullets began to whistle through the air as the Lakota pursued them on foot. Too many were following for Fargo to hope that they'd stay ahead for long. It wouldn't take the warriors more than a few minutes to catch their mounts. Several braves were already riding horses that had been picketed in camp, and they were getting too close.

Twisting while trying to stay in an Indian saddle that was several sizes too small, Fargo fired his Colt. His first shot came close enough to make his target more thoughtful. His second caught another brave in the chest, knocking him down to the ground. His third slammed into a Lakota's shoulder and spun the man hard, but he stayed aboard as his pony halted. The other three reined up, deciding that they could wait for reinforcements before resuming this hunt.

After a couple hours of hard riding, the sun began to sink behind the mountains to the west that men sometimes called the Black Hills. Fargo reined in and slid off his Ovaro, facing the two Santee who pulled up.

"We'll have to fire the prairie," the Trailsman shouted. The Indians understood immediately, but Elizabeth looked even more confused.

She was jaybird naked. Half her hair had escaped from her braids. Tangled and dirty, it framed a forlorn face. While Little Eagle and Red Wolf made little piles of gunpowder and struck flint to steel, Fargo pulled Elizabeth off the pony and wrapped her in a blanket from his bedroll.

"Let's go," Fargo bellowed to the Santee as smoke began to swirl around them. He helped Elizabeth mount a saddled horse. The Trailsman swung atop his own pinto and headed east. It was July and hot. The prairie grasses were thick but dry and quickly roared into flame behind them.

They didn't stop to rest until after it was dark. Red Wolf passed out jerky and hardtack, but Elizabeth didn't eat. She sat away from the others, staring back across the plains.

There was an orange glow on the land, and a sweeping cloud blotting out the dark blue sky. The acrid smell of smoke tinged the air. Fargo went over and sat beside Elizabeth.

He didn't see any way to reach her except bluntness. "Elizabeth, I'm sorry I couldn't get you out of there before they raped you."

"Do you think that matters?" she demanded, spinning to face Fargo. "What difference does that make?" She turned away. "I came out here to help, but instead I risked your life. And look at that," she cried, pointing to the burning prairie. "Some of those people may well be killed."

He turned to Little Eagle and Red Wolf, figuring the one that remembered how to speak English would answer. "You're going back to the Santee country?"

Both nodded. Then Elizabeth said she too planned on returning to Minnesota.

"That's where you're wrong, lady." Fargo grasped her shoulders before she could spin out of his reach.

"What do you mean?"

"I mean you're going to Fort Laramie with me, now."

She bristled and he had to tighten his grip. "I don't see how being held captive by you is any improvement on being held captive by the Lakota," she spat. "You know I must remain there until the allotment comes. Let me go."

"Listen to me, and listen good." Her shoulder muscles lost some of their tension, so Fargo eased his grip, all the while wondering if she was going to knee his balls.

"Elizabeth, there's nothing for you at Ridgely. There's not a damn thing you can do there to help the Santee or anybody else."

"You can't mean that. They're being starved and robbed."

"Their Lakota cousins didn't exactly roll out the red carpet for us," he reminded. "Yeah, your Santee friends are getting crapped on. Maybe they'll decide to do something about it. But the problems aren't all up there in Minnesota, Elizabeth. The Great White Fathers in Washington might clean up that mess if they knew just how bad it was."

Elizabeth dropped her head. "Maybe," she conceded.

Fargo saw his opening and bulled on in. "Maybe you're the one to tell them. You're a general's daughter, a handsome women that speaks well, a missionary—somebody they might listen to. You've done all you can do in Minnesota for the Santee. If you're still fired up about doing something for the Sioux—God knows why after what you've just been through—then go to the people that make the decisions. Tell them how Andrew Myrick and the rest of the traders are robbing the government as well as the Indians."

She straightened, flexing her shoulders. "Perhaps that is what I should do. Then why go to Fort Laramie?"

"To get your father off the warpath," Fargo explained. "You want to help people that are getting persecuted when they don't deserve it? All over the West there are soldiers suffering this very minute—not because they didn't obey orders but because your father will be a prodding, surly son of a bitch until he sees you."

Fargo wasn't sure that what he heard was laughter, but it was close. "He might be even worse after that," she murmured. "Suppose I still choose not to go?"

"If I have to hog-tie you and haul you across the prairie in a travois, I'll get you there." Fargo released her and stepped back. "Maybe that'd be the best way anyway. Whenever I come close to trusting you to do what's sensible, instead of chasing one of your damnfool notions, you sneak away at night or poison my coffee."

She stepped forward. "You wouldn't dare bind me and drag me there."

"It sounds easy as pie compared to trying to rescue you from a Lakota camp."

"After we get to Fort Laramie, I can do whatever I want, go wherever I want?"

"Absolutely," Fargo said. "Fact is, I'd rather you wanted to go to Laramie because you think it's a good idea, not because I'm dragging you there. But if I have to drag you there, I will."

"Mr. Fargo," she spluttered. "I'm an adult and I'm not a criminal. I'm not your wife. You have no claim on me. What right do you have to haul me around hither and yon?"

"I was afraid you'd ask that," the Trailsman answered. He thought for a minute. "Okay, the only way you'll go to Fort Laramie is of your own free will."

"You mean if I head for Minnesota now, you won't try to stop me?"

"I didn't say that." Fargo stepped forward until they were face-to-face. "Let me put it this way. You take off again, and I'll find you again, and we'll have another talk like this one. We'll keep that up until the Indians get us again, maybe for keeps, or until you decide to come with me to Laramie."

Elizabeth leaned forward and embraced the Trailsman. "Skye," she finally said, "I'll go with you to Fort Laramie. But I'm holding you to the rest of what you said."

Her breasts were pushing against his shirt as her relaxed body undulated. "I like the way you hold me," he answered as their hands soothed each other's backs. "But we'd best get going now."

"At night?"

"That prairie fire won't hold them forever. The sooner we can put more distance between us and the Lakota, the more likely we are to get there."

Under normal circumstances, the two-hundred-mile trek to Ft. Laramie from where they were—close to the junction of the Cheyenne and Belle Fourche rivers—would have taken a week, maybe a little longer.

But circumstances weren't normal. No telling how angry the Lakota were after that escape, and these high plains were their territory. The Cheyenne and Arapaho sometimes ventured into this country, too. When whites came through here, they had three options: be killed, usually after torture; travel in a group big enough to discourage attacks; or hide during the day and move only at night. The last seemed the only reasonable course.

Fargo felt like a rabbit that flits from sagebrush to sagebrush while hawks whirl overhead. But smart rabbits survived and so did Fargo as they pushed south to the White River, then westward to the Pine Ridge country. There the prairie grew rough, almost mountainous. They couldn't make more than five or ten miles a night, guided by the stars. But they had more cover, so their resting horses wouldn't be quite so conspicuous during the day. Maybe they traveled without being noticed by the Indians; Fargo could only be sure that they hadn't seen any.

South of Pine Ridge, the going got easier, although the trees vanished and most streams were dry as they neared Ft. Laramie. They were still a good three days away, as the clear sky began to brighten one morning, when Fargo spotted a tiny grove, what had to be the only trees in a twenty-mile circle. As they approached and more light appeared, Fargo recognized a camp—but it was a cavalry detachment, not an Indian hunting party.

Captain James Patterson was probably the spit-and-polish type, since his uniform looked like it was still starched and pressed. But his troopers were rough and disheveled, and the captain sounded reasonable as he warned the soldiers to quit ogling the first woman they'd seen for a spell while some orderlies arranged a hot bath for her. He poured coffee while Fargo answered his questions—at least an hour of them—about the territory they'd been through. Fargo finally got to ask a question of his own.

Patterson nodded. "You're right. We are patrolling quite a bit farther out than usual. Orders from Washington to keep an eye on all the Sioux after what just happened up in Minnesota."

He acted like everybody knew what just happened in Minnesota. But Fargo didn't. Neither did Elizabeth, who emerged just then from the nearby wash tent, using a borrowed officer's greatcoat for a robe. She asked what had happened in Minnesota.

"Can't tell you the all of it," Patterson said, surprised

that they hadn't heard, "because all I know is what came in on the post telegraph. That was quite a bit, though. The Santee went on a rampage. Killed maybe a thousand whites thereabouts, those that didn't get to Ridgely in time to take shelter. Ridgely almost fell before it got reinforced. From the sound of it, it was pure hell inside Ridgely. All those civilians were panicking and begging the soldiers to shoot them before they fell into Indian hands."

"Those ninnies," Elizabeth spat.

"Can't say the military men behaved much better," Patterson said. "You could read between the lines that they didn't have any kind of defense plan for the fort, especially a surprise attack like that."

"It shouldn't have come as any surprise," Elizabeth stormed. "The Santee were starving and the cheating traders' warehouses were full and the traders wouldn't give them any credit. They brought it on themselves."

Patterson slumped back into his canvas field chair. "I suppose so," he concluded. "Look, ma'am. You don't have to tell me what was going on up there. I was stationed at Ridgely until six months ago. But I'm just a soldier. I try to be an honorable one. It's civilians, not the army, that lie and cheat to make their fortunes off some Indians who have precious little to start with. All we get is a chance to die while we clean up the mess they made. So I'd take it kindly if—if you have to get mad at somebody, get mad at somebody besides me."

Fargo thought of somebody. "Any word on what happened to Myrick?"

Patterson brightened. "Tragic," he said, his tone belying his words, "just tragic. Seems he was found dead, his mouth stuffed full of grass and . . ." He noted Elizabeth's presence before finishing the sentence, "his own excrement."

Patterson had his job to do, and so did Fargo. Rested and refreshed by hot meals, they left the camp next sunrise with Patterson's assurance that there weren't any hostiles between them and Ft. Laramie.

Only a day away, they camped early, spreading the bedroll in a spot screened by tall grass.

"What's got into you?" Fargo asked as he watched the woman execute an energetic highland fling. She was naked and her breasts bounced with each jump.

Elizabeth laughed and rolled her eyes. "You've inspired me, Mr. Fargo. I now know what I'm going to do with my life." Her eyes swept his body, and she grew more serious. Suddenly she seemed tongue-tied.

Fargo eyed her warily. He couldn't take her with him. He still had to go see Belle. And afterward? Lately he had been yearning for the wilderness—to get away from settlers, Indians, and government alike. But Elizabeth had been through so much, Fargo wasn't at all sure he had the heart to say no to her if she asked.

"I'm going to become a Free Love lecturer," she announced abruptly. "I'm going to tell everybody about the marvels of sex. And about contraception, of course, so the ladies can enjoy it more freely."

"Good God, why?"

"Why would they want to enjoy sex?"

"No," Fargo snapped. "Why can't you just enjoy sex, and let them do whatever they want? Jesus, Lizzy, you can't be serious. You'll have everybody and their uncles blaming you for all their straying husbands and runaway wives."

"That's not what I'm talking about," she declared. "Free love doesn't mean people sneaking around and cheating on each other. It doesn't mean women doing it just because it's their wifely duty or because they get paid for it or because they'll get beaten if they don't. It means what we've been doing lately, even while we were trying to hide during the daylight. It means men and women enjoying each other."

"That does sound more sensible," Fargo conceded, barely interrupting her speech.

"Mr. Fargo, do you know how many people died in Minnesota? And I've been thinking about those women crowding into Fort Ridgely, women I knew, screaming and begging for the soldiers to shoot them. They were scared to live. Mr. Fargo, I want to live. I want to live because I've never really lived before. I'm tired of being shocked by the world. I'm ready to shock it."

164

"You're really going to do it?" he asked.

"Mr. Fargo, I tried to do the right thing. I tried to warn people that something was happening on the Santee reservation. But no one listened. I have a feeling they'll listen to me now. I'm a fighter, Mr. Fargo, but I'm tired of fighting for food. No one should have to fight for food."

Elizabeth laughed as she collapsed next to Fargo, throwing her bare arm across his chest. "Don't look so worried," she whispered. "I merely mean to take on all of civilized society. I suspect I'll be harassed and probably arrested on numerous occasions, but do you know anyone more suited to withstand those small indignities?"

Fargo lifted Elizabeth's chin and studied her delicate features. "That's really what you want?"

"Oh yes," she assured him, her eyes sparkling. "I want to fight them all. And I want to live, really live. I want to flout all the rules, and be silly and giddy, and laugh a lot, and drive everyone to distraction. For the first time in my life, I want to go forward without looking back. Free love, it does sound nice, don't you think?"

Fargo didn't know what to think, except to be relieved that Elizabeth now displayed a joyfulness and determination that made him almost sorry that they arrived at Ft. Laramie so soon.

The Trailsman had never seen a man with a ramrod stuck up his ass, but he suspected that such a man would stand exactly the same way General Colson stood when he escorted Elizabeth into his temporary office, a corner of the two-story post headquarters on the edge of the parade ground. On this Sunday afternoon they were the only people in the building.

His gray mustache bristled as he glared at Fargo before returning his stare to Elizabeth. "You can leave now, Mr. Fargo."

"No, he can't," Elizabeth asserted. "I want him to stay."

The general's bright eyes, the color of gunmetal, flicked at Fargo.

"Always glad to accommodate a lady," he told the general, his voice level.

"Alright," Colson finally agreed, motioning for them to be seated. "Elizabeth, I must know. Have you finally come to your senses?"

"What do you mean by that?" If the tension in the room got any thicker, he could slice it with a knife, Fargo figured as he watched Elizabeth's back get even stiffer than the general's.

"Have you given up on trying to help those treacherous Santee? You must know that I could have you charged with treason for inspiring them to that dreadful massacre. Will you go back East where you belong?"

Elizabeth stood. "Yes. I've come to my senses, as you put it. I shan't return to Minnesota. I can't inspire massacres nearly as well as cheating white traders can, so I shall leave that up to them in the future. I am going East, father. I intend to become a Free Love lecturer."

She got out the door in time, but that was mostly because General Colson tried to leap over the desk and when he landed, he had Fargo in front of him.

The general tried barking an order to step aside, but that had the same effect military orders usually had on Fargo—none. Then he ducked and rammed his shoulder into Fargo's chest.

Fargo sagged back, bringing round a fist for Colson's ear. The general rocked sideways and tried an uppercut of his own. Fargo blocked that with a chop and realized that the general, even if he had a few years on Fargo, knew plenty about regular boxing. He moved well with smooth footwork, and his array of punches seemed to land without warning. Unlike most generals, who thought that fighting consisted only of issuing orders, this one would get his hands dirty.

The Trailsman back-stepped, hoping for a lunge. The general resisted the temptation and stayed in his crouch, coming forward as smoothly as a ballroom dancer, planting a punishing left jab in Fargo's midsection. Wincing, Fargo sidestepped the next poke and launched himself at the general.

It didn't make much sense to box with a man who was

so good at it, anyway, so Fargo felt more comfortable as he brought the general down with a combined bearhug and trip, then wrestled. Colson muttered something about Fargo not fighting like a gentleman. Then he gave up on it himself, bringing up two stiff fingers for the Trailsman's eyes.

Enraged, Fargo grabbed Colson's hand and twisted. The other hand came up to claw Fargo's ear. The Trailsman ignored it, even when the general started pulling his lobe off. Any second now, the officer was going to recall that he had a sword on his belt, and this fight could get serious.

Looking for some way to prevent that, Fargo spotted a brass spittoon almost within reach as they grappled around on the plank floor. Leaning to grab it meant leaving himself open for a blow that knocked most of the wind out of his chest. Maybe that's why it took two swings of the spittoon against Colson's head before the general gave up on fighting.

Fargo wasn't too surprised the next morning when a courier from the fort caught up to him a few miles down the Platte along the Oregon Trail, where he was just breaking camp.

"Mr. Fargo, General Colson has a message for you," the skinny corporal announced.

"What might that be? Arrest papers? An invitation to the stockade? Maybe a firing squad?"

"No, sir," the corporal stammered. "He said he wanted to commend you on your fighting skills. He said he has great respect for you."

"Well, I thank him for that." Fargo rubbed a sore cheek. "I have some respect for him, too. Anything else?"

"He wants you to find his daughter again. Mrs. Frasier left on the stage yesterday afternoon. He said he wants her stopped before she goes back East and embarrasses the family."

"Then I have a message for the general." Fargo checked his gear. It looked solid, so he swung aboard the Ovaro's saddle.

"What's your message, sir?" the courier asked impatiently.

"Tell him to go piss up a rope."

He was still wondering about what Lizzy would do next when he arrived several days later at the place where the folks in town had said Belle was living. It was a collapsed dugout built into a little ridge, along with a shed made of unpainted, warped planks. But the garden was so well tended that someone must be living there.

An old chicken coop with wire instead of windows, the shed couldn't boast a ceiling more than five feet high. But two dresses hung inside, and a bedroll sat on the dirt floor.

"Belle," Fargo called as he went out back.

"Skye?"

Belle was out behind the corn. Since she didn't come his way, he went to her.

"Belle, what in hell are you doing here?" he demanded as he walked between the rows of tall corn. "I know you like gardens, but surely you could have found a better place."

In a ragged blue dress she stood at the end of the row with her back turned to Fargo. "Goddamn it, Belle. Is something wrong? You could at least turn around and look at me."

"I'm sorry, Skye," she said breathlessly as she faced him. "I'm real glad you're all right. We heard about Minnesota, and that's where you were going, wasn't it?"

"I missed the massacre," he explained before she finished turning. Then he saw her. Belle was as big around as one of her pumpkins. "Jesus H. Christ," Fargo muttered.

Belle drew a ragged breath. "You don't need to look so horrified," she protested. "It ain't yours."

"I can see that," Fargo acknowledged, still staring at her belly. "I reckon that seed was planted back when I was in New Mexico."

"I'm sorry," she cried. "Oh, God . . ."

She was backing up as if Fargo was going to hit her, and she looked terrified. "Belle, why are you apologizing to me? And where did the money I gave you go?"

168

"Tommy," she said. "He's been such a mess. He got hisself in a fight, and they wouldn't let him out less'n somebody paid for the damage. Then he got real mad at me. Said saloons encourage violence and you shouldn't pay 'em for what they'd wreaked."

Fargo sighed. "What are you going to do with the baby, Belle?"

"Tommy says it's his baby," she murmured, folding her hands protectively over her swollen abdomen. "I don't think he likes it none. But he says he won't leave a baby with a woman like me."

"Jesus," Fargo spat. "Come on, I'm taking you to town."

"Tommy won't like it," she objected, backing away from Fargo. "He says he better not hear I've been with a man. Please, Skye, I'm scared. He's been drinking so much. I'm scared he might hurt the baby."

"Fargo," a man's voice called from beyond the shed.

The Trailsman rolled his eyes before turning to stalk back through the corn. "Bradford," he greeted the poet. "How unpleasant to see you."

"They told me in town you were here. You're to stay away from Belle. The woman carries my child, and I won't have her besmirched by your carnality."

"What?" Fargo blurted. "Never mind. I don't want to know. Listen, if you want the woman, you're going to have to fight for her. Because I'm not leaving her in a goddamn chicken coop."

"I don't want the woman. I want the infant."

"Sorry," Fargo said as he slammed his fist into Bradford's belly. "Good warriors have to fight for both."

When the poet straightened, he was wielding a kitchen knife with a long, narrow, double-edged blade.

Fargo fell back to pull his knife from his boot. Bradford had been drinking a lot; he was red-eyed and besotted with rage. He closed in and lashed out repeatedly.

But Fargo was quicker and more experienced. He scratched Bradford's cheek. Then he caught Bradford's arm, and blood flowed down the poet's sleeve. Bradford wasn't daunted. Fargo realized that he might have to kill the man to stop him.

Belle screamed as Bradford jumped back, raising his blade high to plunge it down. Fargo pivoted, ready to go for the man's belly, but he saw the flash of blue. Bradford didn't.

"No," Belle cried, rushing between them. Bradford's blade sliced down. Belle fell back with Bradford's knife buried to the hilt in her shoulder.

"Dear God," Fargo whispered as he caught her.

"I didn't mean to," Bradford whined. "I didn't mean to."

"For God's sake, get a doctor," Fargo roared. He cradled Belle as blood spread across her breast. "Don't die, Belle," Fargo whispered. "Please don't die."

Fargo paced in the doctor's parlor while Bradford sat in a chair, his face buried in his hands. "I'll make it up to her," the poet whimpered. "I love her. I always have. If she had only been different. She never would have sinned with another man. This never would have happened."

Fargo stopped pacing. "Are you talking to me, Bradford?" he asked. "Because if you are, shut up."

The doctor came in. "She'll live," he announced.

"And the baby?" Bradford asked, rising to his feet.

To Fargo's surprise, the doctor turned a lethal glare at the poet. "Get out of here, Bradford. Get out, now."

"But the child is mine," Bradford asserted, his gaunt frame bristling.

"Not anymore," the doctor answered simply.

Bradford turned pale. He glanced at the doctor and then at Fargo, and the two of them glared back. Bradford left.

"She lost the baby?" Fargo asked quietly, realizing what that would mean to Belle.

"No," the doctor answered. He smiled. "Everyone in town likes Belle, but they didn't interfere because they thought she was Bradford's wife. She told me the truth several weeks ago, and I checked into the legality of her situation. Bradford might make a claim, but it would be very weak if the woman is legally married to someone else."

"You expect me to marry Belle?" Fargo mumbled. But then he straightened his shoulders as his resolution grew. "All right. I'll do it."

The doctor stared at him. "No, you won't," he objected. "I'm going to marry Belle."

"You?"

As he saddled his Ovaro, Fargo still couldn't quite believe Belle was getting married. And to a man who actually seemed pretty decent and wasn't too bad-looking. It just wasn't what Fargo had expected, but people had a way of surprising you.

"You know something, horse? Those dingbat transcendentalists had one idea that didn't sound too bad. They say you should commune with nature. That's got to be a whole lot easier than communing with people. Let's go try it." Fargo patted the Ovaro affectionately before he swung into the saddle and headed west.

LOOKING FORWARD!

The following is the opening
section from the next novel in the exciting
Trailsman series from Signet:

THE TRAILSMAN # 79
SMOKY HELL TRAIL

July, 1861, Colorado Territory.
The ramshackle mining camp of Gouge-Eye
boasts of being the roughest town
in the Rockies—and fights
for that right. . . .

"You some kind of sissy, mister?"

Gripping the enameled tinware cup with his massive left hand, Skye Fargo shrugged his muscular shoulders, brushing them with his black hair. The tall man with the full beard lifted his lake-blue eyes from the steaming coffee and the battered pine surface of the bar. He turned to his right for a better look at the halfwit who'd asked the question.

This early on a summer day, the pushy miner standing next to the Trailsman was hard to stomach.

Dressed in the usual garb of patched flannel shirt and baggy wool trousers held up by improvised grass-rope suspenders, the miner wore a bushy brown beard that couldn't hide his lean, wolfish face, or the immense hawklike beak protruding from beneath his beady, porcine eyes. His humorless grin showed missing teeth, and the remaining chompers had faded to a combination of yellow and brown that was about the color of fresh runny sheep shit.

Which was a pretty fair description of the stink that

wafted Fargo's way. The brawny shoulders and hands, though, showed that this grimy saloon idler could feel safe enough whenever he walked up to strangers and started something.

Fargo exhaled slowly through pursed lips, blowing some of the stink away while reining his temper. "Well, if taking baths somewhat regular makes a man a sissy, then I reckon I qualify. Anything else on your mind?"

The oaf shuffled back an inch or two before replying. "It ain't just that. If you was a real man, the kind that gets his due respect hereabouts, you'd start your day with a real eye-opener, a man's shot of forty-rod. You wouldn't sip coffee like some panty-waist."

Fargo allowed himself to quiver a bit and look worried. "Fact is, they didn't have what I wanted," he explained, drawing his words out slowly. "I fancied some tea. In a china cup, with a saucer and sugar and a slice of lemon."

The piglike eyes shifted and the man shot a stream of tobacco juice between Fargo's boots. Sawdust floors were meant for absorbing such abuse. They muffled sound pretty well, too, but not well enough to keep Fargo from hearing telltale shuffles behind him.

When the spitter looked up, anticipation was written all over his grubby face. With another insult or two, everything would be in place. "Tea? You'd try to order tea at the Exchange Saloon? Next thing you know, you'll be looking for a place to squat when you piss."

Fargo felt the silent presence behind him and decided that the time had come to get this over with so he could get on his way.

His left hand rose slowly until the coffee was at shoulder level. His arm sprang like a bullwhip and cast the scalding liquid back into the face of the light-fingered gent who had been reaching for Fargo's wallet.

Just to make sure the would-be thief got the message, the Trailsman swung his long right leg back like a mule on the prod. He didn't need to turn to know what happened because he felt a satisfying squish as his boot heel struck the tender spot where the unseen pickpocket's legs came together.

Before the stinking accomplice in front of him could

get over his surprise, Fargo caught his temple with a roundhouse right. The blow slammed the man's ribs against the bar, sliding him back as his flailing right arm knocked his shot glass and half-drained bottle of rotgut to the floor. He brought up his left for a jab that Fargo deflected. The Trailsman followed with an uppercut that flattened the man's beard and snapped his head back. After that, the gent lost interest in this morning's brawl. He turned and sagged facedown on the bar.

The oily bartender had to have been in on this little game. He'd disappeared the moment that the rawhiding started. Now he emerged from the back room with a bung starter, a two-pound wooden mallet used for tapping the kegs of the vile-tasting concoctions they sold as beer and whiskey. When he saw that Fargo was the only one still standing in front of the bar, the saloonkeeper looked astonished. Things hadn't gone according to the script.

Fargo had fallen for this ruse once, years ago. The idea was to start hoorahing any passing stranger who might have money in his hip pocket. While the stranger's attention was occupied by the insults in front of him, a light-fingered partner would approach from behind and lift his wallet. The bartender, who got a cut of the proceeds, would keep things orderly. Usually he stepped in before matters got violent between the stranger and the insulter.

This bartender swallowed hard and gave Fargo a thoughtful look. "I'll not have fighting in here," he announced.

"See anybody fighting? I don't, and I've got pretty good eyes." Fargo stepped back to be sure he was out of the hammer's range.

"You can't just come in here and abuse my good local customers," the bartender proclaimed as he noted one patron scrunched up in the sawdust and the other drooping face-first on the bar top. He stepped forward to lay his bung starter under the bar.

"Likely they are good customers. I'm sure they stay right here to spend most of what they steal."

His hands remaining behind the bar, the round-faced man tried to stay expressionless. "You sure ain't easy to get along with, stranger. You come in here and prod me till I make some coffee. Then you start a fight, and now you're saying my saloon is a den of thieves. I don't rightly know how much more of this I'm supposed to take.''

Doubled up in the damp sawdust next to the bar rail, the slender pickpocket began to stir and straighten. Fargo ignored that and kept his eyes pinned to the bartender.

''You'll take your hands off that goddamn scattergun you're fixing to pull up,'' the Trailsman announced as his hand settled on the grip of his Colt.

But maybe they all really did believe that he was a sissy. Because the bartender seemed to think that he could bring up the sawed-off double-barreled shotgun and cut the stranger in half before the Trailsman could draw his Colt and punch a .44-caliber hole just above the man's button nose.

The bartender was wrong about that. He lacked time to consider that error, since his last act was a reflexive pull on the triggers as he fell back. Fargo had sprung forward with his own shot, so he was crouched against the bar as the twin explosions thundered just overhead.

Double-ought buckshot sliced through the barroom. Most of the lead plunked into the primitive roof, a bunch of skinny poles topped with dirt. Dust and mouse turds rained down through the powder smoke as Fargo started to rise, then noticed some twitching in the nearby legs of the gent who'd started all this with the question about morning coffee.

The Trailsman grabbed the nearest leg and jerked it hard, down and away, slamming the man backward to the floor. Had the surface been anything stouter than sawdust, that would have been enough. But the man twisted one leg free while kicking furiously with the other. With his back to the bar, Fargo didn't have much room for dodging, so he caught one bruising hobnailed boot in his chest. Gasping as he crabbed along the bar, away from those striking boots, Fargo got to the knocked-out pickpocket.

The slender thief was starting to sit up and take notice. He stood up when Fargo grabbed his collar and trousers from behind and straightened. Then he got to fly as Fargo spun round once to gain momentum before launching the man, who seemed almost as light as his fingers.

His husky friend was just starting to stand and reach for his pistol when the pinwheeling pickpocket smashed into his belly. Both went down in a cursing heap of thrashing arms and legs.

Fargo stepped easily to the plank door. Perhaps it was time to move on before anybody else in this town asked another damn fool question. . . .